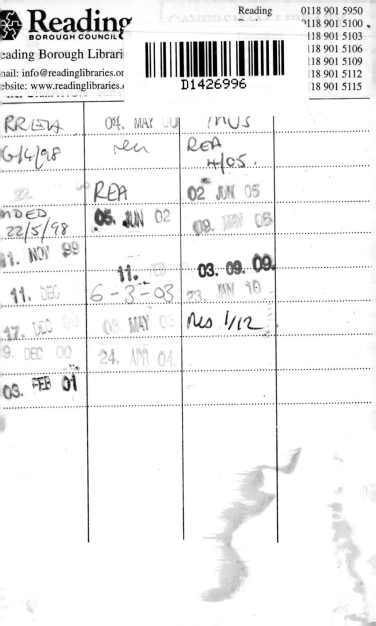

From a background of social science and education, Joe Cooper has been interested in folklore and the symbolism of fairy stories for many years. He is the author of *The Mystery of Telepathy*, *Astroverse* and *Modern Psychic Experiences*, and has contributed on the paranormal to the *Guardian*, *New Society* and provincial newspapers. He has participated in many radio and television programmes and lectured extensively on psychic studies. After running adult evening classes and dayschools in psychic studies for ten years, his main concerns are the sociology of knowledge and the benefits of soulfully revived psychology at physical and social levels.

He has been a member of the Scientific and Medical Network for six years and lives at Headingley in Leeds, West Yorkshire.

The Case of the Cottingley Fairies

Joe Cooper

POCKET
BOOKS

LONDON · SYDNEY · NEW YORK · TOKYO · SINGAPORE · TORONTO

Published in hardback by Robert Hale Limited, 1990

First published by Pocket Books,
an imprint of Simon & Schuster Ltd, 1997
A Viacom Company

Simon & Schuster Ltd
West Garden Place
Kendal Street
London W2 2AQ

Simon & Schuster of Australia
Sydney

A CIP catalogue record for this book is available from the
British Library.

ISBN 0-671-01026-3

Typeset in Garamond 10/12pt by
Palimpsest Book Production Limited, Polmont, Stirlingshire
Printed and bound in Great Britain by
Cox and Wyman Ltd, Reading, Berkshire

This book is dedicated to
two amiable adventuresses

ELSIE AND FRANCES

❦ Contents ❧

❧ *Contents* ❧

But remember always, as I
told you at first, that
this is all a fairy tale
and only fun and pretence;
and, therefore, you are not
to believe a word of it,
even if it is true.

Charles Kingsley
The Water Babies (1863)

❧ Picture Acknowledgements ❧

Glenn Hill: 1–3, 5, 7, 13, 16–17. The Brotherton Collection, University of Leeds: 6, 10, 21, 26. Geoffrey Hodson: 25. All other illustrations from the collection of the author.

❧ Foreword ❧

by Colin Wilson

In one single spectacular investigation, Joe Cooper has achieved what every student of the paranormal dreams about: a permanent place in the history of psychical research.

The Cottingley sensation erupted in the Christmas issue of the *Strand* magazine for 1920, with an article by Conan Doyle on the 'fairy photographs' taken by two Yorkshire schoolgirls. The sceptics howled with laughter, declaring that they were obviously cardboard cut-outs. Doyle and many others defended the existence of 'natural spirits' and argued for the genuineness of the photographs. But within a year or so, it had all been forgotten.

In the mid-1960s, a journalist discovered that the girls were still alive, and went to interview the eldest, Elsie Wright. She declined to say if the photographs had been faked, saying she preferred to 'leave it open'. That certainly sounded ominous. Joe Cooper, a Yorkshireman, made it his business to meet both girls, and pressed them hard. In an article in a magazine called the *Unexplained* in 1981, he quotes them as standing by their original story. But by the following year he was able to follow it up with an article in which the girls – both now old ladies – described how they had faked four of five photographs.

If that was all there is to it, it would hardly be worth writing a book about it. In fact, the story is far more fascinating and complex. My own investigations into the paranormal have brought me into contact with a number of people who insist that they have seen 'natural spirits', and I am inclined to believe them. That is why I believe that the story reconstructed by Joe Cooper in the present book is as near as we shall ever come to the complex truth behind the case of the Cottingley fairies.

One thing is quite clear: Joe Cooper has written a book that will become a classic in the annals of psychical research.

✳ Acknowledgements ✳

I should like to thank the Brotherton Collection Librarian at the University of Leeds, Christopher Sheppard, for allowing me access to the Cottingley material and for permission to reproduce the Conan Doyle letters and the photograph of a younger Geoffrey Hodson trying to discern fairies.

I am very grateful to Glenn Hill for his permission to use the five photographs originally developed by his grandfather, Arthur Wright, and also for the sketch and painting executed by his mother, Elsie Hill.

My thanks are due to the undermentioned:

To the Theosophical Publishing House for permission to quote from the works of Edward Gardner and Geoffrey Hodson.

To Peter Holdsworth of the *Bradford Telegraph and Argus* for permission to quote from his article on Elsie Hill.

To Century Hutchinson Publishing Group for permission to quote from *Your Psychic World A to Z* by Ann Petrie.

To the Literary Trustees of Walter de la Mare and the Society of Authors as their representative for permission to quote an extract from the poem 'The Fairies Dancing'.

To the Society of Authors as the literary representative of the Estate of Rose Fyleman for permission to quote the poems 'Smith Square, Westminster' and 'Fairies'.

To the Estate of F. Scott Fitzgerald, the Bodley Head and Macmillan Publishers Limited for permission to quote from *The Great Gatsby*.

I have made every effort to identify copyright holders and to obtain their permission but would be glad to hear of any inadvertent errors or omissions.

Joe Cooper, January 1997

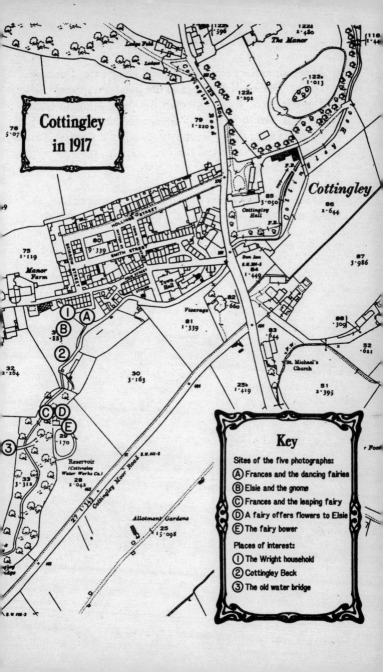

Cottingley in 1917

The Manor

Cottingley

Cottingley Hall

Manor Farm

HOLLINGS STREET
SMITH STREET
JOHN STREET
Town Hall

Vicarage

St. Michael's Church

Reservoir
(Cottingley Water Works Co.)

Allotment Gardens

Cottingley Moor Road

Ⓐ
Ⓑ
②
Ⓒ Ⓓ
Ⓔ
③

Key

Sites of the five photographs:

Ⓐ Frances and the dancing fairies

Ⓑ Elsie and the gnome

Ⓒ Frances and the leaping fairy

Ⓓ A fairy offers flowers to Elsie

Ⓔ The fairy bower

Places of interest:

① The Wright household

② Cottingley Beck

③ The old water bridge

Prologue

Childish Wishful Thinking and Probabilities

For those intrigued by the bizarre and fashionable subject of psychic studies (in which fairy experiences particularly appeal), may I recommend a book by the American adventurer Herbert O. Yardley entitled *The Education of a Poker Player*. He lived a colourful life from 1889 to 1958, during which time he was active in diplomatic espionage, notably the decoding of some 200,000 Japanese coded messages in wartime. He also occasionally assisted the Chinese government, enjoyed hectic social episodes and was buried with full military honours at the end of his days.

Although his absorbing interest was winning at poker, he was endlessly intrigued by human foibles, notably in the matter of probabilities as opposed to childish wishful thinking – what on balance was likely to be the truth of matters, as starkly exposed on card and casino tables the world over. For misguided gamblers will often persist against steadily lengthening odds, ignoring all data, logic and inferences. Stakes pile up and they are unable to heed or assess accumulated evidence, so that over-optimistic attitudes, reminiscent of the young perhaps, persist in the face of ultimately demonstrated reality.

I would suggest that those who ignore the data of accumulated psychic phenomena from the past century or so incline more to the category of wishful thinkers than realists. Evidence is in by the boatloads for seemingly questionable notions such as telepathy, clairvoyance, astral travel and personality survival at death. The sceptics – mostly atheistic conjurors and materialistic psychologists – choose to ignore (or know not) such disinguished authors as Bozzano, Doyle and Barrett from the earlier part of the century and Crookall, Monroe and Inglis from our own times. Personal reports, labelled as subjective or anecdotal, have generally been ridiculed by those who assign credibility to knowledge in our society, and the uneasy are shadowed by black magic, Ouija boards and 'dabbling in the occult'.

Ghost stories, in particular, have come under heavy critical fire, often being consigned to the category of illusion or 'good stories made better'. Guy Playfair, however, writes pithily on this point in his recent book *The Haunted Pub Guide*:

> You might think that all pub ghosts can be ascribed to alcohol-induced hallucinations. You would be wrong. People tend to exaggerate anything they think likely to enhance their self-image, such as the size of fish caught, speed of a Jaguar reached in first gear, or number of women seduced. Yet to claim to have seen a ghost does not generally do anybody's reputation any good. Most people who have such experiences tend to keep quiet about them.

Such is certainly true in the case of those who have seen or heard fairies. I have tape-recorded some score or so from those who have experienced a variety of nature spirits, and a frequent comment is that they have kept silent for fear of ridicule.

So it was with Frances, the girl at the very centre of the Cottingley story. It was in the summer of 1917 that she first saw fairies down at the beck and, apart from telling her cousin Elsie, kept quiet about it. Only an irate mother continually scolding and slapping her for falling in the stream and getting wet eventually forced a sobbing confession from her.

It is at this point that our fairy-story begins, but it may be instructive to return to Yardley in order better to appreciate what followed. The analogy between poker and social life, with its bluffs and strategies, may be closer than most imagine. We all try to gauge probability, and we mostly think wishfully, childishly or otherwise. We compete for glory, prestige, power and material advantages; and each day brings us a different game and cards in our hands, where we seek survival and enjoyment in the immediacies of everyday life from hour to hour.

My tale thus involves humans and their ways as much as sprites, notably how they react to unusual psychic and social situations. Emotionally based belief systems underpin such reactions, and the unfamiliar is often distorted to accommodate prevailing habits of thought within the context of ongoing knowledge systems. But here, of course, I run the danger of missionarizing for sociology, the second most important card I was dealt in my own particular lifegame. (The first was the certainty, from infancy, that we are both body and soul.)

* * *

At the centre of the affair, of course, were Elsie and Frances, the charming heroines to whom this book is dedicated. They are now otherwise occupied, Frances departing in July 1986 at almost eighty, and Elsie following at eighty-six in March 1988. Both, I like to hope, will be somewhere without, encouraging their tattered clown as he taps out his words, even though I blew their cover in December 1982, helped by Fred Gettings. Our articles appeared in the *Unexplained*, issues 116/7, and the ladies owned up in early 1983 in *The Times* and elsewhere.

In my fancy I see them flanking Herbert O. Yardley, the trio raising glasses of ambrosia, for Out There can always make mincemeat out of Time, Space and Matter if it so chooses. The toast, of course, is stumbling humanity with all its imperfections – me, you and all of us the world over.

Back, then, to Cottingley 1917 and the arrival of a nine-year-old Frances Griffiths with her mother Annie from the sun of Cape Town, while her father went to the war and Europe where he might employ his gunnery expertise. As for his little daughter, she was to come to the cold and April snow of the village; which was, perhaps, to stay silently in some quiet place of her heart for more than sixty years.

Beginnings (1917–30)

❦ 1 ❧

Cottingley, 1917

Two village kids and a practical joke that got out of hand.

Popular verdict on the Cottingley Fairies

Cottingley, now a well-populated suburb of Bradford, has always been much more than the little village often described by commentators. It was, even in 1917, more urban than rural, in spite of its appearance, for it boasted a town hall, of all things, a mechanics institute and a mill – outstandingly unusual features of any village life.

Neither were Elsie and Frances typical 'village kids'. Each was an only child, unusual in those days; both had travelled to distant places in their infancy. Frances had been born in Bradford and journeyed out to Cape Town when very young. And when Elsie was four, her father, Arthur Wright, had fallen out with his millionaire boss Mr Briggs and sought his fortune in Canada with his family for four years, helping to build houses. He had been missed so much that his former employer had sent Arthur the fares home, and peace was made between the two, as Arthur returned to his old job of electrical and motor maintenance at the Briggs' Cottingley mansion. When Elsie came back to Britain, she had a Canadian accent and was teased about it; when Frances arrived in April 1917, she had a South African accent and found village life strange after the lush social life associated with being the only daughter of a senior NCO where there had been servants and weekly visits to the opera wearing her small cloak trimmed with fur. So both were not only socially experienced as girls but also had known what it was to be singled out for derision, long before the photographs came along.

By 1917 a certain grim resignation, if not disillusionment, had begun to set in. The year before had been the Battle of the Somme and, more out of curiosity than anything else, I looked up the headlines of July 1916 on the 'Daily British Advance' and John Buchan describing 'the superb achievement of our armies in shattering the German Western Line'. Then had come the lengthening casualty lists, the mute photographs of the slain in the *Telegraph* and *Argus*, and the feeling of wondering about it all.

Frances recalled visiting a young soldier whom she would pass on her way home from school each day, sitting outside in a summerhouse extension of the house where he had come to die, after months of suffering in the squalor and wet of the trenches. She remembers his smile and stoical cheer, and the abruptness of the day when he was no longer sitting there at the open window to greet her.

Many of the women in the village had menfolk fighting.

Annie, mother of Frances and sister of Polly, actually became bald with worry about her soldier husband as the months dragged by, and took to wearing a wig. And one day a neighbour came across to Polly with a saucepan full of pea pods. 'I've boiled these', she confessed ruefully, 'instead of the peas. I was thinking of our Edwin in France, and chucked 'em away on the midden . . .'

In the Wright household there was warmth and humour. Polly and Annie had come from the raucously happy Curtis family, where their bold father, a carpenter and entrepreneur generally, was given to singing uproarious ditties of a doubtful nature. The more sober Arthur Wright, after visiting the house for the first time to ask the formidable redheaded patriarch for the hand of his daughter in marriage, had laughed so much at the spontaneous vulgarity to piano accompaniment that his ribs ached all through the next day.

On some occasions when friends visited, a wide-eyed Frances would watch intrigued as Annie held forth in serious conversation, jumping with laughter as her mother would suddenly whip off her wig and reveal a bald and shining pate, to the astonishment of the listeners. ('I pity anyone around with corns when Frances gets excited,' wrote Annie in a letter once.)

Then there was the local pride of Cottingley which, as has been said, was no ordinary village. During the Great War *Cottingley Town Hall and Sunday School Centenary Souvenir 1814–1915* had been printed for circulation generally and perhaps particularly for soldiers away from home. It was indeed a proud hundred years record, and I bought it when by an odd coincidence it chanced to be in a Bradford secondhand bookshop in the very week when I first started writing this chapter.

The aggression of aspiring Cottingley is there behind the short and stern prose:

> Can we picture to ourselves the England of 1815? The population was only eleven million souls ... Gas was practically unknown. A member of Parliament got up in the House and said 'You might as well talk of ventilating London by windmills as talk of lighting streets by gas.' Duelling was common. Intemperance was an everyday fault. Laws were severe. Men could be hanged for stealing a sheep. The prisons were in a dreadful state. Women could be flogged in public places. One person in every eleven was a pauper.

Remorselessly was the proud Victorian progress of the old village detailed: the day school was founded in 1865, with the Mechanics Institute starting in the same year; in 1870 the town hall was built, and thereafter followed the Band of Hope, the Choral Society, the Independent Order of Rechabites and Cottingley Women's Guild in 1904.

It is thus, as far as I know, the only village in the country to boast a town hall and a Mechanics Institute. Such venerable buildings are still to be seen on Main Street, and it is indeed odd that a place with a population of only around 1,500 achieved such minor splendours. It certainly reflects much enterprise and unity, and also an underlying appreciation of the benefits of favourable public presentation, and of being as good as anyone else, perhaps.

This Yorkshire competitiveness was also marked among individuals in the village. Arthur Wright, for example, in addition to his various technical skills, was one of the best chess-players in the area and took on all comers. On one occasion a formidable opponent from afar was found for him in the person of a deaf and dumb man who, it was reported, was unbeatable. Arthur lost the first game by an early slip, and the other indicated that he did not wish to compete further against such easy opposition. However, he was persuaded to stay, and Arthur went on to beat him again and again as the evening lengthened. At the end of it all, the visitor rose to his feet and, with enormous difficulty, enunciated the only word anyone had ever heard him speak, so it was said later. 'Boo ... boo ... ger,' he managed to get out, before leaving ungraciously with his supporters.

On another occasion, Frances has a vivid recollection of next-door neighbours vying with each other as to who could get the washing out first on a Monday morning. One had stooped to putting hers out the night before, to be met with vicious abuse from her competitor, as the latter came out of the house with her basket of clothes to be pegged up. A wordy exchange and escalating insults continued, the climax being when the loser seized a shirt tail and unkindly pointed out traces of excrement – a certain sign of slovenly washing. The other, however, shrilly claimed this to be an iron burn.

Thus ideas of the time and the place, and the spirit of its inhabitants, might be built up. The so-called Yorkshire character is indeed a strange amalgam, stemming from the Brigantes of Queen Cartimandua, the Romans, Saxons, Danes, and their struggles for survival and domination. The bloodiest battle in English history was fought at Towton Field on Palm Sunday in 1461; in 1644 Marston Moor saw the conflict between Cromwell and the Cavalier; and the more or less continuing struggle between masters and masses has continued ever since, Scargill's flying pickets being but a pallid modern reminder of more violent confrontations. One might comment that assertive males such as Messrs Close, Boycott, Illingworth, Savile and Parkinson are but inheritors of a long tradition of independent thought and action – a mode of orientation irritating to many in the south, but a source of glee to those born in the Broad Acres.

For the county produces more comedians than most others. The deadpan jest, the sharp ones masquerading as simpletons, the lampooning of the socially stuffy – all these strands are to be found. As, oddly, is an interest in matters psychic, for spiritualism first took a public hold in the West Riding in the 1860s, and in 1917 religious attendances were significant in all recognized churches, and also at such fringe institutions as the Theosophical Society in Bradford, favoured by Polly and Annie.

Such, then, was the social backcloth against which 17-year-old Elsie and 10-year-old Frances came to take photographs which were to puzzle the world for more than sixty years.

❧ 2 ❧

Frances and the Fairies

'There were fairies at Cottingley.'
Frances in her last television appearance in 1986

To raise the question of a belief in fairies, with most people, is to invite ridicule. The very term 'a fairy-story' suggests some sort of fabrication, and the whole idea of nature spirits (or elementals or any other name by which they may be known) is linked with childhood and fiction.

In fact, evidence for humans having seen fairies is, at least in the view of many seasoned psychical researchers, quite good. Consider a comment made by William Riley, author of the best-selling novel *Windyridge*: he knew the Yorkshire dales well and maintained that he had come across several people who had 'many times seen pixies at certain favoured spots in Upper Airedale and Wharfedale'. Baring Gould and Halliwell Sutcliffe are other writers who have collected accounts of fairies having been seen in Yorkshire. So human experience of fairies, at visual and aural levels, is perhaps not as ridiculous as might be thought.

But Frances Griffiths, aged nine in the summer of 1917, knew nothing of people having seen fairies in the Yorkshire dales.

The beck at the bottom of the long garden of 31 Main Street fascinated her from the start. It was, and is, a very unusual feature of the village, for driving along a nearby road one sees a stretch of fields with tops of trees appearing to rise suddenly at a midpoint. Such a physical feature indicates that the distant beck is comparatively narrow and has very steep sides: these slope down sharply some fifty feet, and the old water bridge spanning the banks is only a matter of thirty yards or so in length. In consequence, the beck is strangely enclosed and drains down quietly to the Aire, under the road going down to Bingley, about half a mile away. During the first year of Frances' stay in Cottingley, she and Elsie would often spend hours at the beck, an appealing and private playground.

Frances was always an extremely perceptive and artistic person, as was Elsie. Only in her later years did she come to realize that others could not necessarily share her aesthetic appreciation of the beauties of nature. She wrote to me in 1977 describing her first experience of an English spring:

I was running to Bingley from school, to save the half-penny fare as usual, and the sun was shining – the first time, it seemed, for months ... and suddenly, when I reached the Parish Church, I saw Spring. A pale blue sky, tree branches thickening with a promise of pale leaves soon and the world was a wonderful place. A long time afterwards I read Winifred Holtby describing how I felt at the time with the words, 'When I die, nobody will ever again know that particular sweet fierce exaltation which stirred the rapturous, unblurred imagination of the child.'

Our eager and bright 9-year-old would race home from school at Bingley, toss her satchel down and go along the garden path to the beck. In those days foliage was rather more overgrown than now, and there was a waterfall not far from the end of the garden. Frances would pick her way among the moss and stones, at one with the sunlight on the sparkling waters or the lush spring greenery. She was always quite certain that the beck was at the very centre of the whole episode of the fairies, and often suggested to me in our brief spell of abortive authorship together that our book title should be based on the glittering stream. We spent some time trying to think up some vivid phrase but our efforts usually dissolved into failure – and laughter at the more ridiculous attempts, the sense of humour of the older Frances being sharp and prominent.

Her account of the first time she ever saw a nature spirit – in this case an elf – was particularly interesting. She told me that many times on her solitary visits she had noticed single grasses or leaves moving vigorously; inexplicably, for the foliage around would not be in motion. (It is true that on most days there was something of a breeze at the beck, but not such as to cause swift and sudden movement in but a single blade of grass.) Here is what she said about first seeing a nature spirit:

One evening after I came home from school I went down to the beck to a favourite place – the willow overhanging

the stream . . . then a willow leaf started shaking violently
– just one. I'd seen it happen before – there was no wind,
and it was odd that one leaf should shake . . . as I watched,
a small man, all dressed in green, stood on the branch with
the stem of the leaf in his hand, which he seemed to be
shaking at something he was looking at. I daredn't move
for fear of frightening him, but just sat looking at him.
He looked straight at me and disappeared.

Now here, of course, we come to a division of readers into
believers and non-believers. The former would say that
this seems a straightforward and honest, if not intriguing,
account of the sudden appearance of a nature spirit and
that Frances, with a biography of honesty, should be given
the courtesy extended to most in everyday conversation –
that she is telling the truth about what she saw and that
we should accept this, albeit at a subjective level. Others,
perhaps, would not see the little man, but Frances did.

Psychologists, however, might talk in terms of 'nego-
tiable evidence'. They would put forward the simple
statement that very few (if any) see little green men shaking
leaves by the side of streams. Therefore Frances was
perhaps hallucinating, imagining that the green patterns
formed a little man or that some physiological feature of
her mind's eye seemed to project into reality in some way.
Darker cynics might say she was lying for effect, hoping
for some financial or publicity advantage – or even to get
attention, this being a common need of younger children,
of course.

Much, of course, depends upon individual reading and
experience. As will be seen in the case of Arthur Conan
Doyle and Edward Gardner, to whom the whole area of
nature spirits was of abiding interest, people who have
seen fairies have begun to record experiences and build

up pertinent literature. So an account by a girl of seeing an elf holding a leaf by the side of a stream around which grew oak, thorn and ash – the traditional fairy trees – might well be tentatively accepted. Conversely, if nothing has been read by critics on the subject of fairy-sighting, scepticism is more likely.

From then on, astonishingly as it must seem to most, Frances saw more of fairy life beside the beck on other solitary visits. The most common among the nature spirits seemed to be 'little men, dressed in green, wearing long green stockings, coats of greyish green and matching caps', who often used to hurry along the pebbly edge of the beck. They would sometimes skip across the stream and disappear into the grasses. Often they would appear to Frances to be watching her closely.

The elves, she commented, always seemed to be purposeful in their movements, as if engaged on some urgent task. She deduced that in some way they help with plant and vegetation growth, and this accords with other accounts I have heard from medium friends of mine, who have seen devas (large nature spirits) around and among trees. The settlement at Findhorn in Scotland also has many believers in fairies, who point to the lush growth of the fruit and vegetables grown, as they are suggestive of nature spirit encouragement. Opportunities for further reading on this matter, to say nothing of research, abound.

As the summer of 1917 lengthened, Frances saw more and more nature spirits. She saw fairies with and without wings, looking much as they are depicted in illustrations in fairy books. This is, oddly, a source of wonder to some – that fairies should look like fairies. Yet if fairies *have* been seen down the years, fanciful illustrations will relate to traditional stereotypes, which themselves may be based on real sightings of nature spirits.

She noticed that the fairies were smaller than the elves and had white faces and arms. They would sometimes sit in groups in patches of sunlight and give the appearance of holding a meeting of sorts. The prevailing atmosphere would be one of peace, said Frances, and she would hardly dare move for fear of disturbing them. They seemed to notice her but were apparently unsurprised by her presence: 'Sometimes they would come up, only inches away, and I always felt it would be spoiling things if we tried to join in their lives. The little people always seemed to be busy with their own affairs . . . it was a happy time up the beck, with always the sound of water running over the stones and glimpses of fairies.'

Frances saw fairies far more often than 'the little men', and they seemed to be sprightlier altogether than the elves.

'They were very pretty and such fun to watch,' she once told me, and I noticed a certain gentleness about her when she said this. Doubters might well point to my gullibility (I believed in the authenticity of the photographs for five years, and I generally trust people and expect them to be truthful rather than not), but I can understand her profound fascination with the running waters of the beck in the sunlight and associations with fairy folk.

On the subject of whether she talked much about fairies to Elsie, she was oddly reticent. By 1917 she would be coming up to ten, to Elsie's sixteen; they were close companions and would often disappear for hours 'up the beck', taking sandwiches and drink with them, and it is likely that Frances would tell her cousin of what she had seen. Frances told me and others that Elsie 'never saw fairies', and it may have been that such was the case, for the perception of fairies is, as far as is known at the moment, an extremely rare capacity.

Yet in 1911, years before Frances came to Cottingley, Elsie had been absorbed by fairies, notably in a water setting. Such a preoccupation is unusual by any standards, even given the prevailing atmosphere of Tinkerbell, Dulac, Arthur Rackham and the rest. In her teens her painting skills grew, and her own appreciation of the beck is well evidenced in a passage from a letter she wrote to me in 1977: 'The view from the little bedroom at the back part of the house always seemed very lovely, especially on moonlight nights, and being an end house right on the highest spot of the village the wind used to make a lovely musical sound around the corner where I slept. I missed the sound of the waterfall at the bottom of our garden when we moved to our new bungalow in 1921' – and of the beck, before Frances arrived: 'It was so peaceful and it had a sort of feeling about it . . . I used to spend hours there just watching the birds . . .'

Frances and Elsie were thus both absorbed by the beck, which had an unusual charm all of its own. It is clearly possible for the imaginative to interpret shades of light, or the movements of birds or leaves, as being more than such. This, of course, is the most common explanation for ghosts – tricks of the light, and lively imaginations at work. Plus the ever-present need for vivid stories, so that good tales become even better in the telling; amused listeners use such euphemisms as 'over-enthusiastic' and privately imagine the experiencers of spectres or fairies to be deluded.

And now for a point which may be of interest to those who favour the methods of Sherlock Holmes, whose shadow was always over the whole affair of the Cottingley Fairies. (Due tribute is paid to him in the Epilogue.)

Speaking of the appearance of the first little green man she saw, Frances commented, 'Once I fancy he became visible in order to see me eating an orange – a rare delicacy in wartime.' And on another occasion, 'I once heard, I believe, a little man playing on a pair of pipes, but when he played them the sound was so high pitched that I could hardly hear it, and it sounded no more than a ringing in my ear.'

Let us imagine, for the moment, that Frances never saw any kind of elemental life by the beck but was making it all up. What would she say? Conceivably, there would be talk of odd leaves and grasses moving, for such reports in nature-spirit setting are comparatively common, and she might have read or heard about such. Again, she mentions connections between streams and running water in the sunlight and fairy life, and this, too, could have been gleaned from fairy books by an intelligent and well-read girl like Frances. But it is very unlikely that she would fabricate the matter of the orange or the sound of the pipes being almost inaudible; one making a good tale better would go in for haunting melodies on the sunlit air, with perhaps elves and fairies dancing delicately all round.

Another interesting point is that on the tram to and from school at Bingley, Frances would imagine a group of 'little people' just like ourselves, only inches high, living in a world of fun and excitement. 'Now and again,' she once said, 'I had to join in the fantasy world and become really bossy.' Such daydreams on the tram continued through the summer of 1918 but then stopped abruptly.

Another significant straw in the wind came in a letter from her to me in 1978:

About a month ago an old friend of mine came to visit me. We were girls together and she astonished me by telling me how I used to show her signs of fairies' presences. She said she could still recognize a fairy sun bath after I'd shown her all those years ago! I'd completely forgotten I'd shown her anything, but as she was my trainee clerk (I was 18 at the time and the shorthand typist on a building contract) . . . she talked about things I'd forgotten and I now remember vaguely. I've asked her to write it all down and send it to me when I can get down to a book . . .

And Frances also told me that for some time after Cottingley she could see vague shapes 'at the sides' in country places, and this accords with the experiences of others I have met, who claim to have seen nature spirits from the 'corners' of their eyes.

Frances was basically a very private and dignified person who did not welcome publicity. On the walls of her Ramsgate home she had landscape pictures that she had drawn at home and overseas, and she also, like Elsie, modelled in clay. One of her most sensitive works is that of a young clown's head, which somehow reveals her innate capacity for empathy with others and for appreciating the vulnerability and humour that may be found in such a performer.

'It reminds me of you,' she told me once.

'You flatter me. I'm a failed song-and-dance man at heart,' I replied. 'With a dash of the cheery thug intellectual.'

This last comment proved apt, for our last encounter was as adversaries. She rang on New Year's Day 1983. Some three weeks before, I had published an article in the *Unexplained* giving the truth of the photographs. The year before, I had updated the case in three articles, and since the magazine was scheduled to finish in the spring of 1983, I judged it my duty to see that bona fide occult students should be the first to know of realities. By then Elsie, Frances and I were pursuing independent courses of authorship. Neither of the ladies wanted me to be the first to reveal matters, but I had gone ahead on the advice of others besides myself.

I picked up the phone, and a distant voice said 'Hallo?' I recognized the tone as that of Frances.

'How nice to hear from you, Frances . . . a very Happy New Year to you . . .' Too much gushing again, I thought. Why do I gush to Frances?

A pause. Then, 'Oh, it's you, is it? I wanted to speak to your wife.'

'Ah well . . .'

'You're a traitor.'

And slam – down went the phone.

Somewhere Out There, hopefully, she has forgiven me and perhaps will smile down upon her admirer as he tries to tell her story.

3

First Photographs

I know none of us will come out of this very well,
but it started with the best of intentions and Elsie's
wish to keep me out of continuous trouble. Only
smacks and scoldings and all my own fault, but
I couldn't do what my mother wished — to keep
away from the beck, or if I went upstream, not to
get my expensive black shoes, long woollen stockings
wet every time.

A note to the author from Frances, September 1981

In the early summer of 1917 Frances had seemed obsessed with going down to the sparkling stream at the bottom of the garden and, being rather clumsy, had sometimes lost her footing on slippery stepping-stones, finding herself suddenly sitting, dolefully, in a foot of tumbling water, soaking her lower clothing, black stockings and shiny shoes. Her mother had been furious. Time

and time again had Annie Griffiths slapped and scolded
her daughter, but still she persisted in going to the beck
– and getting soaked.

There had been the time when Aunt Polly, Annie's
sister and Elsie's mother, had joined in the interrogation
in support of Frances's irate mother.

'Yes – why *do* you keep going to the beck so often,
Frances?' demanded the sharp-eyed Polly.

A silence. Then, cornered by the grown-ups, she burst
into a flood of hot tears and blurted out, 'I go to see the
fairies! That's why – to see the *fairies!*'

There had been surprise and then a strange silence, with
a clear atmosphere of total disbelief. Then Elsie came to
the defence of her cousin and said that she, too, had seen
the fairies.

But the grown-ups scoffed at it all.

Let the words of Elsie, sixty years later, take up the
story on tape; her words are best reproduced in the
cadence of free verse:

> She cried bitterly I know
> I said, 'Let's go up the beck'
> I was trying to think of something
> To get her mind off the troubles
> And then I said:
> 'Well, these fairies we see
> Well, let's take a picture'
> I didn't think we'd go on with it
> It was just to take her mind off things
> But she got this into her mind
> She kept on about it
> She livened up and said:
> 'Oh yes, let's try and take one.'

And so
After being nattered a bit
I said we'd do it.

Thus one Saturday afternoon in July 1917 Elsie asked her father if she might borrow his Midg camera, in order to take a photograph of Frances, down by the beck at the end of the long garden.

Arthur Wright was reluctant. He had bought the camera only a month before, and Elsie had never taken a photo in her life. Glass plate negatives were also in short supply, and the banks of the beck were slippery, as were the stepping-stones giving a path of sorts across. But in the end his gangling, beautiful seventeen-year-old daughter talked him round. There was a strong bond between them. Elsie admired her father, for his was the success story of a lad who had started work at nine in the grim mills of Bradford in the 1870s and had slogged away to become skilled at a variety of trades before coming to work for the millionaire Briggs at his Cottingley mansion, where he maintained the five splendid motor cars.

He showed her how to use the tiny viewfinder, put a glass plate into the camera, and away went Elsie with nine-year-old Frances to take the first photograph of her life – a photograph which was, over the next few years, to become one of the most vigorously debated in the whole strange history of psychic photography.

They were back within the half hour and eager to see the plate developed. Arthur had built a makeshift dark-room under the cellar steps in the house at the end of Main Street, having recently acquired chemicals, a developing-tray and other materials needed to produce negatives and positives in those early days when photography was becoming available to a wider public.

But it was after tea before he finally got round to obliging the two cousins. Elsie squeezed herself into the cubbyhole, with Frances outside, pressed eagerly against the door, listening to the conversation.

First of all Arthur saw some odd shapes coming up on the glass plate, as he manipulated it in the tray. There was the face of Frances, elbow resting on a convenient bank as she stared at the lens of the camera, but around were these . . . they looked like sandwich papers. He began to chide Elsie for being untidy down there at the beck, when the wings began to appear and the thought that they might be birds occurred to him. And then, when tiny legs and arms appeared, he fell silent.

Elsie was excited. 'The fairies are on the plate!' she called out to Frances, on the other side of the door, and there came a squeal of delight and the sound of gleeful skipping on the stone flags outside.

Arthur Wright now found himself looking at the outlines of flowing hair and what seemed to be pipes.

His verdict was immediate and definite. 'You've been up to summat,' he judged brusquely.

When, later, the sepia print was produced and more details could be made out, it seemed a surprising picture indeed. The wings of the shapes were blurred and seemed to be five little figures dancing beneath the unconcerned face of Frances. A waterfall was there in the background, as were mushrooms. It was an odd first snap for anybody to take.

But Arthur still dismissed it as a joke. Cut-out fairy figures, probably, for Elsie was good at art (having thankfully left school at 13½ for the art college in nearby Bradford) and she had been drawing fairies for years. Those who had been at the village school with her, years before Frances and her mother had come to stay with the Wright family, remembered how she would draw figures in the margins of the textbooks and in autograph albums. But then these were the days of Arthur Rackham and Edmund Dulac, to say nothing of Peter Pan and Wendy. Even so, throughout her girlhood Elsie had been interested in the world of trees and landscapes, and at seventeen she was a water-colour artist of no mean ability.

'They're fairies!' insisted Elsie, to her parents and her Auntie Annie, mother of Frances.

Frances agreed with her cousin. 'Now you can see', she told the grown-ups, 'why I have been going up to the beck so often.'

'Yes – now you *have* to believe Frances,' said Elsie.

The mothers of the girls, Polly and Annie, didn't know what to make of the snap. They had always known their daughters to be truthful, and the repeated statements that there *were* fairies had a ring of truth about it. Both ladies were coming round to being interested in Theosophy and were interested in the possibilities of a life beyond and nature spirits on earth.

However, after a week or two the fuss died down, without the girls disclosing any further details. The two Yorkshire characteristics of deadpan drollery and a liking to be one up on others may have come into matters, they thought. Or perhaps . . .

August lengthened into September, and Arthur Wright's camera was borrowed again, this time for Frances to take a photograph of Elsie up by the old oaks on the northern bank of the beck, where the astonished Arthur was to see a gnome, of all things, in the sepia print from an over-exposed plate. His daughter's hand was oddly elongated, which Frances assured her uncle was caused by the way in which she held the camera, this having been the first time she had ever taken a photograph. Both girls affirmed that gnomes were often to be seen there, as in the photograph.

After that, Arthur refused to lend them the camera any more. The two prints were copied and recopied over the next year and became something of a novelty among the family and friends, as both the cousins stuck firmly to their story of the truth of fairies being at the beck – and having been photographed.

The Great War came to an end. Armistice celebrations and parades were extensive, as in the village, where a robed Elsie was cast as Victory riding on a converted farm cart, with Frances and other loyal representatives at her feet. She had a rough ride (the shape of things to come?), as she wrote in a letter to me: 'I had a laurel wreath round my head and held a long golden trumpet to my lips, but the hard cart wheels on the bumpy village roads made it impossible to put it into my mouth without knocking my teeth out. I kept clouting myself across the eyes and nose all the time. There were others on the cart to represent the various services. They were having a much steadier time of it . . .'

It is possible that the whole affair of the fairies would have faded away had it not been for Annie and Polly taking an interest in Theosophy and going to crowded meetings in Bradford at Unity Hall in Rawson Square in 1919.

On one occasion a lecturer mentioned fairies, and

Polly approached her at the end of the lecture and asked whether it was possible that some fairy pictures taken by her daughter and niece the summer before might be, as the girls had repeatedly maintained, true after all.

From that point on, our odd tale becomes odder still.

4

The Man in the Bow Tie

'Are the photographs genuine, Mr Gardner?'
'I'd stake my reputation on it.'
                              E.L.G. in conversation at a
                              Theosophical meeting in 1921

If there is to be a prince in our fairy-tale, let it be Edward L. Gardner. He was handsome enough, with his bow tie and beard, and respected by all. He lived out his century from 1870 to 1970, and the coming to his notice of the Cottingley photographs at the half-way point in his life was the making of him: from it he was to gain a stature in the Theosophical Society which was to boost him for the rest of his days and enhance his reputation at his lectures around Britain and on his 1927 tour to the USA ('CHAMPION OF ELFS STRUTS HIS STUFF,' declared a *New York Evening Post* headline.)

In the end, at seventy-five, he managed to bring out a book all of his own on the matter, with Arthur Conan

Doyle long since dead. It was called, somewhat lengthily, *A Book of Real Fairies: The Cottingley Photographs and their sequel*. Alas, it did not really live up to its promising title for little new had been added to Doyle's book, *The Coming of the Fairies*, gathered twenty or more years before. Nevertheless, it was reprinted several times and has come to be regarded as the last word on the strange case. Phoebe D. Bendit wrote an introduction to the 1966 edition and commented: 'Whatever one may conclude about the validity of the photographs, one thing is beyond doubt: the complete integrity and objectivity of the author.'

Certainly his other works, published, like this book, by the Theosophical Society, indicate his loftiness of endeavour:

> *The Heavenly Man*
> *The Imperishable Body*
> *The Play of Consciousness*
> *There Is No Religion Higher Than Truth*
> *Thyself Both Heaven and Hell*
> *The Web of the Universe*
> *Whence Come the Gods*
> *The Wider View*

Gardner first came to see the prints after copies had been passed to the Bradford Theosophical Society in 1919. Besides having crowded meetings every Wednesday at Unity Hall in Rawson Square, the society was hoping to expand and add another lodge to the two smaller ones on the outskirts of Bradford. The missionary impulse flourished indeed.

After the grievous Great War, interest in other planes

to which the fallen had departed ran high. Polly declared that Theosophy 'rescued her from atheism', and she would often go to the Unity Hall lectures, sometimes with Annie or Elsie. A Theosophist who was in his twenties at the time well remembers audiences of 200 or so coming along. He does not remember Polly or Annie but once met Elsie when the affair was at its height: 'I have a distinct memory of talking to Elsie Wright in the lecture room of Unity Hall, Rawson Square in Bradford. She was a tall girl with auburn hair and blue eyes . . . she seemed to take the fact that she'd seen fairies as something normal. She wasn't at all thinking it was something miraculous. She didn't seem particularly interested in talking about it. She couldn't understand what all the fuss was about.'

Edward Gardner was the President of the Blavatsky Lodge in London and also a partner in a jobbing building business, having worked his way up from being a carpenter. He travelled the country giving lectures at various lodges, and my informant remembers conversing with him at Bradford once: 'I had a great respect for him. If you asked him a question, he'd give you an answer in absolutely precise terms. He had a very clear mind.'

Inevitably, he had asked Gardner whether he thought the fairy photos genuine.

'I'd stake my reputation on it,' he declared. Most Theosophists also shared his opinion, as did some London photographic experts of the day who had scrutinized plates and prints.

Thus did Gardner first become involved.

Some months after members of the Bradford Lodge had prevailed on the Wright family to part with the glass negative plates and the sepia prints which had been stuffed away in a drawer and forgotten as a joke of some kind (to which the girls, for reasons unknown, had never owned up), Elsie's mother received this letter early in 1920:

5 Craven Road
Harlesden. N.W.10.
Feb 23rd 20.

Theosophical Society: Lantern Slides
Dear Mrs Wright,

I have just seen a photograph of 'Pixies' that Mrs Powell has, and she tells me it is through your little girl that it was obtained.

I am very anxious to make a collection of slides of such photographs for the society's work and am writing to ask if you can very kindly assist me. The print I have seen is certainly the best of its kind I should think anywhere, and if you can help further I shall be greatly obliged. Perhaps you would be so kind as to answer the following queries . . .

E.L.G., as many called him, detailed such questions as Who, Where, What and How and concluded with:

I am keenly interested in this side of our wonderful world life and am urging a better understanding of nature spirits and fairies. It will assist greatly if I was able to show actual photographs of some of the orders. Of course I know this can only be done by the help of children at present and am delighted to get into touch with such promising assistance as it seems your little girl can render. Very sincerely yours, Edw. L. Gardner.

Now Polly was of modest education and may have been somewhat over-awed by the headed notepaper and type-writing. Accordingly, she sought the assistance of a lady whom she had met, shortly before, at her neighbour's

house. The lady in question, to return again to the theme
of coincidence which runs like some mysterious thread
through our tale, was a Mrs Wright, like Polly, but was
no relation. Her first name was Edie and she lived at 145
Manningham Lane. Importantly, she was better educated
than most at the time and had been a member of the
Bradford Theosophical Society but had left for 'private
reasons'. She was also diminutive, even by prevailing
Cottingley heights, smoked a clay pipe (a habit acquired
from her grandfather as a girl), played cricket and could
render Beethoven pleasantly on the piano.

When writing to Gardner in 1946, seeking a copy of his
book and commiserating with him on the loss of his house
in the blitz during the war, she recalls how she came to
meet the Wright family:

The lady living next door to the Cottingley Wrights
introduced me to them one evening and after Mr and
Mrs Wright had gone off to a choral practice there was
left in their house Elsie, Mrs S. and myself. The piano lid
was open and I ran my fingers over the keys. Elsie asked
me if I could play for her. I played some Beethoven. Elsie
gave a sigh and said 'That was lovely.'

We then at once began to talk about fairy photographs
and during the conversation Mrs S said, 'I wish you'd take
me up the beck, Elsie, to see the fairies.' Elsie said, 'The
fairies would not come out for you in a hundred years.'
'Take Edie, then' meaning myself, said Mrs S. After that
evening I often went on to Cottingley to see the Wrights
and to talk Fairy lore with Elsie and her mother . . . Mr
Wright always remaining unbelieving and ending up by
saying 'They must have done summat.' Then came your
letter of questions to Mrs Wright and she asked me to
answer it.

Correspondence between Edie Wright and Gardner flourished. The pipesmoking cricketer gave full details as to when and where the photos were taken, and stated that both mothers believed their daughters' story of real fairies being photographed, even after more than two years. She also retrieved the negative plates from the Bradford Theosophists and sent them to him for inspection – and improvement, as it happened. The original sepia print of Frances and the fairies was clearly substantially retouched.

Gardner was perfectly open about sharpening outlines, as he wrote in a later letter to Doyle: 'I begged the loan of the actual negatives – and two quarter plates came by post a few days after. One was a fairly clear one, the other much under exposed . . . the immediate upshot was that a positive was taken from each negative, that the originals might be preserved untouched, and then new negatives were prepared and intensified to service as better printing mediums.'

He also gave other instructions, as he mentioned in a later letter to the secretary of a Birmingham society concerned with studying supernatural pictures: 'Then I told them to make new negatives (from the positives of the originals) and do the very best with them, short of altering them mechanically. The result was that they turned out two first class negatives which of course are the same in every respect as the originals except that they are sharp cut and clear and far finer for printing purposes.'

Gardner wrote to Edie Wright asking if Elsie might take some photographs on her forthcoming holiday, saying that he would be only too pleased to provide a camera and plates for her. His prose verges almost on the Elizabethan: 'If I may beg you to favour me so far do you think you could arrange with Miss Elsie to attempt some photographs of fairies in Ireland? Should she not already be possessed of a camera I will very gladly send her a good hand Kodak . . .'

His copy letters are in purple and are firmly and accurately typed in the Brotherton collection of the Cottingley Fairies correspondence in the Brotherton Collection at Leeds University library. (By another odd coincidence they happened to arrive there in 1973, the year in which I just happened to begin my investigation in the matter, working at my home perhaps only a mile away – astoundingly convenient.)

March lengthened into April, and Edie Wright travelled to Ilford to see friends. She broke her journey at London and, in the rooms of the Theosophical Society, Gardner met the tiny Yorkshirewoman. There she told him of the way in which the girls stuck to their story and how their mothers believed in them. However, the voluble Edie also passed on erroneous information, such as the girls having played with fairies since 'babyhood' – an obvious exaggeration.

Gardner also sought out one Harold Snelling, who had recently set up on his own as a photographer. He made careful enquiries as to the bona fides and abilities of Snelling and was told by his former employer, with whom he had worked for years, that, 'What Snelling doesn't know about faked photography isn't worth knowing.'

E.L.G. sought him out and presented him with an original sepia print for inspection, together with the plate from which it had been taken. Snelling put the plate on a glass-topped table and illuminated it from below. He then took a number of lenses and minutely and lengthily examined the mute-faced Frances and the sprites around her.

His considered judgement, again taken from Gardner's 1945 book, was firm and surprising indeed: 'This plate is single exposure,' he remarked. 'These dancing figures are not made of paper nor of any fabric; they are not painted on a photographed background – but what gets me most is that all these figures have *moved* during exposure . . .'

It was no wonder, then, that in May Gardner was showing lantern slides of the first two photographs with some degree of assurance. It was at Mortimer Hall that his cousin, Miss E. M. Blomfield, saw the pictures, and Arthur Conan Doyle was one of the people she informed as to their fairy content. By yet another coincidence, Doyle had been asked by the editor of the *Strand* magazine to write an article on fairies for the Christmas number in 1920, well before he had known anything of the Yorkshire photographs. As he was to write later: 'The evidence was so complete and detailed, with such good names attached to it, that it was difficult to believe that it was false: but being by nature of a sceptical turn, I felt that something closer was needed before I could feel personal conviction . . . following up the matter from one lady informant to another, I came at last upon Mr Edward Gardner.' (*Strand*, Vol.IX, no.31, p.403)

So it was that the creator of Sherlock Holmes met his real life Watson, and our curious case began to move along even more swiftly.

❧ 5 ❧

Watson – The Game is Afoot!

*I saw Sir Oliver Lodge and showed him the photos –
we are both sufficiently on our guard already.*
Letter from Doyle to Gardner, 3 July 1920

In June 1920 Arthur Conan Doyle (an internationally known and highly respected figure) met Gardner for the first time. He had been knighted for services as a medical officer in the South African war, and he had a reputation for fiercely championing causes in which he believed, whether it was the reform of divorce law or opposing formidable Bernard Shaw, who wrote deprecatingly of Captain Smith for having carelessly lost his ship, the R.M.S. *Titanic*. But, at sixty, his burning cause was spiritualism, and he was interested in all matters pertaining to Higher Orders – including fairies.

Doyle was best known, of course, as the creator of Sherlock Holmes; indeed, the very phrase itself has been used so often in connection with him that it is in danger of becoming a cliché. But even though more than thirty years had passed since he had written 'Sherrinford Holmes' on the blotter of his desk at Southsea while waiting for patients who only seldom came, the by then world-famous author, as might be expected, moved cautiously after seeing the two photographs. He must have known that E.L.G. would be delighted to have gained the attention of one of the most eminent men in the land, and his first letter was crisp and business-like:

> Windlesham
> Crowborough
> Sussex
> 22nd June 1920

Dear Sir,

I am greatly interested in the 'fairy' photographs which really should be epoch-making if we can entirely clear up the circumstances. I am going to Australia presently to lecture on psychic matters, and I should much like to get copies, not for exhibition but for private use. It so happens that I am writing an article on Fairies at present, and have accumulated quite a mass of evidence. It will appear, I think, as one of 'The Uncharted Coast' series in the *Strand*. I would willingly pay any reasonable sum, say £5, to reproduce the pictures and this would be a good way of getting them formally copy-righted both in England and America, which I certainly think the father of the girls should do.

If I might have one or two notes as to who he is, where he dwells, the age of the girls, whether they are in other ways psychic and so forth, it will greatly help me in my description.

We are all indebted to you as the channel by which this has come to the world.

Yours sincerely.

A. Conan Doyle.

Gardner wrote back with enthusiasm. He had been experiencing difficulty in persuading Polly and Arthur to let Elsie take further photographs. Arthur, in particular, had expressed a mixture of puzzlement and irritation, feeling that there was something strange about the whole affair, although Polly believed in real fairies being photographed (as subsequent correspondence with Gardner and Doyle was to show). From these differing parental opinions, it is clear that both Frances and Elsie had stuck to their story for almost three years – but the whole episode had been comparatively brief, soon forgotten and dismissed as some curiosity.

E.L.G.'s response to Doyle's letter shows how easy it is to pass on unchecked information:

> June 25th
> Your interesting letter of the 22nd June has just reached me and very willingly I will assist you in any way that may be possible ... the children who are concerned are very shy and reserved indeed ... they are of a working class family in Yorkshire and the children have played with fairies and elves in the woods near their village since babyhood ... the two are far better than one as the proximity of the aura as you probably know strengthens the very delicate etheric vehicle of the fairy and make it more acitinic ...

It was agreed to meet at the Grosvenor Hotel for lunch and discuss the matter. We can imagine the two of them: Doyle at sixty, large, with a suggestion of the military man, and Gardner ten years younger – smaller, bearded and eager to assist. Their conversation must have been lengthy, with a thorough examination of such data as were then to hand – to bring in, yet again, the shadow of Holmes.

Much would hinge on the testimony of two people: Mrs Edie Wright and Harold Snelling. The Beethoven-playing fairy-enthusiast would have spoken to E.L.G., perhaps, of her conversations with Elsie and the Wright family, of the belief of Polly and Annie in their daughters, and the scepticism of Arthur. Gardner would have described the care with which Snelling had examined the plates and prints, and the latter's insistence that the figures had moved would have cropped up. There would also be the matter of motive – why *should* the two (seemingly uncomplicated village girls) go to the sophisticated extent of fabricating figures? And obviously to do such would entail much careful work and perhaps copying from a number of books. How *could* such girls have the skills for this, to say nothing of the privacy and opportunities for trial and error – Gardner would mention that Polly and Arthur had carefully searched the girls' bedroom for any traces of paper cuttings and had also walked alongside the beck in such a quest. There was also the matter of setting such figures in position – how *could* they be suspended in mid-air, for example?

Both men had much experience in examining psychic photographs and were familiar with ideas of ectoplasm exuding from around the heads of mediums in which figures often built up. Contrary to popular belief, there are hundreds of genuine photographs indicating such forms; the massive work of Schrenck Notzing and Richet of France demonstrates the genesis and appearance of ectoplasmic forms conclusively enough, although current British scholars choose to ignore such potent source material. And, in the first sepia print of Frances, there are apparent ectoplasmic whisps around her head.

There is also the account by Gardner of how the

photographs came to be taken. In his book, written a quarter of a century later, he describes it thus, and it is fair to infer that the first account given to Doyle at the Grosvenor would not be substantially different: 'It was on a Saturday at the midday meal that there had been some bantering about "The Fairies" and Elsie retorted "Look here, father, if you'll let me have your camera and tell me how it works I'll get a photo of the fairies. We've been playing with them this morning . . ."'

Doyle was to describe E.L.G. later as 'quiet, well balanced and reserved – not in the least of a wild and visionary type'. It was further decided that Gardner should go north and interview the Wright family and the cousins ('the personal side of the matter') while Doyle should 'examine the results and throw them into literary shape'.

On 30 June Doyle raised the matter of money with his Watson: 'If you go the *Strand* magazine would, of course, pay your expenses and say £25 more for the interview . . . why should you not get paid for such work . . . ?' He also enclosed a personal letter for Gardner to pass on to Arthur, and a covering note regretting that his Australian trip prevented him from coming to Cottingley to see Elsie:

Dear Mr Wright,

I have seen the very interesting photos which your little girl took. They are certainly amazing. I was writing a little article for the *Strand* upon the evidence for the existence of fairies, so that I was very much interested. I should naturally like to use the photos, along with other material, in my article but would not of course do so without your knowledge and permission. It would be in the Christmas number. I suggest:

1. That no name be mentioned, so that neither you nor your daughter be annoyed in any way.

2. That the use be reserved for the *Strand* only until Christmas. After that it reverts to you.

3. That either £5 be paid to you by the *Strand* for temporary use, or that if you don't care to take money you could be put on the free list of the magazine for three years.

The article appears in America in connection with *Strand* publications. I would, if you agree, try to get another £5 from that side. If this is agreeable to you I or my friend Mr. Gardner would try to run up and have half an hour's chat with the girls.

Yours sincerely.

A. Conan Doyle.

The strategy worked well. By 14 July Gardner was thanking Polly for her kind letter inviting him to come and visit the Wright family towards the end of July.

It is difficult for us today to imagine the greater rigidity of the class structure sixty years ago. Besides obvious differences of language, apparent at the sound of the first sentence uttered by anybody, there were subtleties of manner, actual volume of voice, clothes and habits of hygiene which are less divisive today. However, relative ways of deferring to this or that person – 'knowing the right boots to lick' is perhaps a crisper expression – are with us as much today as they ever were. 'Nobody can help a brigadier on with his overcoat like a public schoolboy,' wrote Muggeridge tellingly, once, I seem to recall. As in former savage days, we allow ourselves to be dominated in order that we are protected and thus survive.

So it would be that Polly and Arthur would receive the

well-clad Edward Gardner, gravely bearded and bow-tied after the fashion of H. G. Wells and others, with a measure of respect. There would also be, somewhere, perhaps, the creeping feeling of having ventured into deeper waters, which would inevitably transmit itself to Elsie. The original prints were there – blurred and indistinct, notably that of the gnome, where a young Frances had over-exposed light on the plate. And, very importantly, nobody could ever check on the past incident. All hinged upon the word of Elsie and, to a much lesser extent, on that of the younger Frances.

On this occasion, in July 1920, Frances was living in Scarborough with her soldier father, who was stationed at Catterick after having been decorated in the war and attained the rank of regimental sergeant major, in which position he was a rigid and feared figure.

Gardner interviewed the Wright family at length.

Since Polly was very interested in Theosophy at this time, no doubt Gardner would dwell upon realms of higher consciousness and worlds different from our own, perhaps to the irritation of Arthur. Polly and Elsie would be there together, and the latter would endorse her statements made earlier, perhaps after the manner described by my Theosophical friend, who shared the conviction of most at the Bradford lodge that the snaps were what they purported to be according to Elsie.

Gardner walked down to the beck with Elsie and verified the spot where she had taken the first photo by the waterfall. He had a photograph of himself taken there, perhaps feeling, oddly, that the mushrooms by him, as in the photo of Frances, somehow confirmed matters: if Elsie was so truthful and straightforward about the site which could afterwards be verified, perhaps the photographs . . .

He stayed overnight at the Midland Hotel, enjoying media hospitality which is even more lavishly extended to those with newsworthy stories today. The following day he talked again with Polly and Elsie, took the tram back to Bradford from Cottingley Bar, and so to London and 5 Craven Road, where he immediately, and carefully, wrote up his report for Doyle, helpfully making purple carbon copies, so that we may read his words today.

He wrote in sure terms as to the authenticity of the first two photographs: 'Extraordinary and amazing as these photographs may appear I am quite convinced of their entire genuineness.'

Doyle, however, was less certain, as indicated by phrases in letters to E.L.G.:

[3 July:]
I saw Sir Oliver Lodge and showed him the photos . . . we are both sufficiently on our guard already . . .

[5 July:]
I let Kenneth Styles who is a fairy authority see the prints. He was suspicious. 'If my surmises are correct,' he writes, 'one at least is a most patent fraud and I can almost tell you the studio it came from . . . the coiffures of the ladies are much too Parisienne . . .'

[18 July quoting again from Styles:]
'The more I think of it the less I like it . . .'

[7 August:]
Per contra our enemies might quote that roughness of one shin bone, as if the tool had not cut true and unfinished look of the hands. If I were *sure* on this point I would not have a shadow of doubt in the world . . .

Here, indeed, has the Holmesian side of Doyle surfaced – regrettably momentarily, for if he had spent
time investigating what he considered, on the one hand,
the 'epoch-making event' but, on the other, not important
enough to warrant a journey to Yorkshire, he would
surely have penetrated the impassive comments of Elsie.
As it was, he was immersed in his preparations for his
Australian departure in mid-August. This, in itself, is
another odd coincidence. In a hurried postcard (a popular
form of communication at the time) he indicated the
pressures on him: 'Things have become a procession now.
I find I have 1½ hours clear on Wednesday. If you lunch
with me at the Grosvenor Hotel at 1.30. then you can go
on to the city . . .'

So Doyle departed, leaving Gardner to go north yet
again and obtain more fairy photographs from Elsie and
Frances, both of whom were now supplied with good-
quality cameras and plenty of plates. These latter had
been marked by Illingworth but, incredibly, not accounted
for on return, so that the exact number of photographs
developed from plates could not be known.

The results obtained in the last three photographs were
to please both investigators, to cause one of the mightiest
controversies in the history of psychic photography and
to start off a mystery that was to last for more than
sixty years.

6

Further Photographs

P.S. She did not take one flying after all.
Polly Wright in a letter to
E.L. Gardner, August 1920

By the early August of 1920 Edward Gardner must truly have felt himself to be riding on the crest of some benevolent wave: Doyle, while not totally accepting the two prints of the Yorkshire fairies (as they were generally known then), had involved himself in the affair and, thanks to his correspondence with the Wright family, had secured permission for E.L.G. to visit Cottingley with the idea of taking more photographs; also Gardner's report on the apparent genuineness of the photos and Arthur and Polly had been praised by Doyle, and there was talk of book-publication in the air, in addition to the article to come out in the Christmas number of the *Strand*, in which Doyle was to give preliminary details of the 'epoch-making event'.

Doyle felt the need for further proof. On 10 August he wrote to Gardner, suggesting that he should get an affidavit. 'We would send a paper with a sixpenny stamp simply worded,' he wrote, but, rather mysteriously perhaps, the matter was dropped. There are many interesting reasons, of course: Elsie was an 'infant' at law, and her parents could hardly swear to that which they had not seen and so forth – it is curious that talk of affidavits, swearing on the Bible and similar assurances of veracity have constantly been sought from Elsie over the past decade, but until 1983 she resisted them all. Surely, if her story of real photographs had been true, she would not have hesitated. Thus it is by what people do not do, rather than by their actions, that truth might often be deduced; although here it has taken (yet again!) the wisdom of hindsight to realize this, at least on the part of fairy-supporters.

Frances recalls how Gardner came to Scarborough, to which the Griffiths family had moved after her father's demobilization in 1919, and talked of sending a camera and plates to her, to be used in the second fortnight of August, when she went to Cottingley.

He came up and he just spent an hour or two with us. I always remember him coming up. We sat down to dinner – my mother had cooked him fried eggs and chips, and she told him very carefully that it had been cooked in butter ... [for the important visitor was a vegetarian, like many Theosophists who did not wish to pollute their systems with meat.]

I had no real impression at all of him ... he was just an uninteresting person in brown with a brown beard and brown hair and a brown suit who had nothing much to say ... and it made it very difficult for a little girl to talk ... I had been brought up to make conversation with people – to keep the conversation going ...'

Now here is a very interesting sidelight on the disposition of Frances as a girl. She had grown up in the fairly rich social life of a senior NCO's household in Cape Town, where talking to servants, socializing and mixing with adults were commonplace experiences – as were frequent outings and mingling in adult company. Thus, early on in her life, she came to appreciate the need to present herself favourably – and also when to be discreet and keep quiet. Add to this that her father was a Yorkshire stoic of a sergeant major, whom she saw often and who influenced her much in her early years, and there is the picture of a young girl well suited to keeping her mouth shut if the need arose – as it did.

Elsie, too, had travelled abroad as a girl, had mixed widely and was close to her parents, but Frances describes the relationship between Polly and her daughter as '... friendly but not affectionate – the Curtis family didn't go in for kissing'.

Frances described her meeting with E.L.G. as follows: 'It was very difficult with him. They left me alone with him for about ten minutes and then came and rescued me – he was just scrambling a few notes together ... he wasn't scientific at all.'

This account of the meeting may be balanced against that of Gardner in his book written in 1945:

The trip to Scarborough proved satisfactory. I interviewed Mrs Griffiths and Frances, both then seen for the first time, and a half hour's talk with Frances explained a good deal. The girl, at that time thirteen years old, was mediumistic, which merely meant that she had loosely knit ectoplasmic material in her body. The subtle ectoplasmic or etheric material of the body, which with most people is very closely interwoven with the denser frame, was in her case unlocked or, rather, loosened, and on seeing her I had the first glimpse of how the nature spirits had densified their own normal bodies sufficiently to come into the field of the camera's range.

Alas, we must charitably assume that Gardner used his refined powers of perception to establish the nature of the etheric body of Frances, for she recalls no conversation with him on the matter. In fact, Frances knew fewer psychic experiences in her life than Elsie.

Frances mentioned that 'there is a dispute over the number of plates ... I think he sent us six packets of plates ... because there seemed to be an awful lot ... he said "practise with them so that when you go to Cottingley you'll know what to do" ... so I took him at his word ... I was taking photographs of all my friends ... my school ... my mother said "you'd better save them" – so I had to stop taking photographs ...'

Polly had gone out for the afternoon, and in a letter to Gardner on Sunday 22 August she describes her side of the affair. It is in neat handwriting, sloping evenly to the right, reflecting precise and repetitive board school instruction in Bradford in the 1880s, and the tone of the letter also suggests the respect of the skilled working class for their 'betters'.

She writes of the afternoon of Thursday 19 August 1920 thus: 'The morning was dull and misty so that they did not take any photos until after dinner when the mist had cleared away and it was sunny. I went to my sisters

for tea and left them to it. When I got back they had
only managed two with fairies. I was disappointed.'

The last sentence is important. It shows that Polly
believed, as she was to all her life, that her daughter and
niece both saw and photographed fairies at Cottingley.
Gardner and possibly Doyle would be impressed with
her candour and faith, and they would doubtless make
the assumption, as have many others, that links between
mother and daughter are usually of a totally honest nature
and that Elsie had confessed to her mother what they
imagined to be the truth of the matter.

An addition to Polly's letter further underscores her
belief in the authenticity of the first two photographs,
which, in the summer of 1920, had been held for a
matter of two years without having been shaken in the
slightest. The sentence runs: 'P.S. She did not take one
flying after all.'

The first two plates were developed by Arthur and
prints taken. I can find no record whatsoever as to how
Polly and Arthur reacted to these, but by now important
people were involved, money and time had been spent
by Gardner and Doyle, and any retractions at this point
would truly have resulted in considerable embarrassment
all round and unpleasant consequences for both Elsie and
Frances. Both girls maintained that fairies had been seen
and photographed; Polly applied Theosophical reasoning
and accepted the photographs at their face value; Arthur
fell silent, and his liking for Arthur Conan Doyle declined
sharply, Elsie often told me. Up until that point he had
expressed admiration for the eminent author, but ever
after he revised his high opinion of that spiritualistic
missionary.

On Saturday 21 August 1920 the girls went to the

beck and walked around by the old reservoir, but it was a dull and drizzly day. Here is an extract from a letter to Gardner from Polly, giving details: 'They went up again on Saturday afternoon and took several photos but there was only one with anything on and it's a queer one, we can't make it out. Elsie put the plate in this time and Arthur developed it the next day.'

Descriptions of how the photograph came to be taken differ between Elsie and Frances. Elsie claimed to have taken it on her own, in *The Times* interview of March 1983, whereas Frances maintained that *she* took it in the company of Elsie. She described how she and Elsie were 'mooching about in mackintoshes at a loose end' and said that Elsie had 'nothing prepared'. They made their way a little upstream, where they had not often been before, and Frances told me that she saw figures building up in the grasses and took a photograph, the result being a 'jumble up'. At the time of writing this (July 1988) the matter awaits clarification, but it does seem that Frances had an imperfect recollection of the event; as she herself said, some details have become clouded.

Gardner, in 1947, of course, goes into enthusiastic details as to exactly what is happening:

Fairies and the Sun-bath
This is especially remarkable as it contains a feature quite unknown to the girls. The sheath or cocoon appearing in the middle of the grasses had not been seen by them before, and they had no idea what it was. Fairy observers of Scotland and the New Forest, however, were familiar with it and described it as a magnetic bath, woven very quickly by the fairies and used after dull weather, in the autumn especially. The interior seems to be magnetized in some manner that stimulates and pleases.

56

There is thus still mystery left in the case of the last of the photographs. Who was right? Elsie or Frances? For one or the other must have been mistaken, and only further close photographic analysis may clarify matters.

Edward Gardner, of course, was delighted at the last three photographs. He telegraphed immediately to Doyle in Melbourne as to the success of the enterprise and must have been pleased indeed to receive the following from the great man:

> October 21st
> Dear Gardner,
> My heart was gladdened when out here in Australia I had your note and the three wonderful prints which are confirmatory of our published results . . .
> When our fairies are admitted other psychic phenomena will find a more ready acceptance . . . we have had continued messages at seances for some time that a visible sign was coming through . . .

Here, of course, Doyle scoffers will have a field day and state that this, indeed, is evidence of the waning of his critical powers. Yet many others were convinced by these last three photographs. Consider, for example, two comments made by Fred Barlow to Gardner; the former was a leading authority in the country on psychic photography and, in particular, faked photographs. These two letters, at a distance of months, show his attitude sharply changed:

> [28 June 1920]
> I am inclined to think, in the absence of more detailed particulars, that the photograph showing the four dancing fairies is not what it is claimed to be . . .

[12 December 1920]

I am returning herewith the three fairy photographs you very kindly loaned to me, and have no hesitation in announcing them as the most wonderful and interesting results I have ever seen.

Fred Barlow.
Hon. Sec. Society for the Study of Supernatural Pictures.
Birmingham.

So was Doyle heartened by the news from home. In Melbourne he wrote to Gardner: 'My work goes rarely well. The soil is parched and drinks it all in. Plenty of breezy opposition too.'

His first article in the *Strand* Christmas number in December was to be greeted by even more mixed, and tumultuous, reactions in London.

❧ 7 ❧

The Strand *Articles*

An epoch-making event.
  Strand magazine cover heading for December 1920

T he bright Christmas number of the *Strand* came out
  at the end of November 1920 and was sold out within
days at most outlets.

Doyle's article 'Fairies Photographed' was given headline prominence on the familiar front cover, and such other
popular writers as Sapper, Wodehouse and Oppenheim
were relegated to minor displays amidst the *Strand* background scene. Arthur Conan Doyle had been a popular
writer for the magazine since there had been published in
it some thirty years before, for the first time, the Sherlock
Holmes stories. Now the war was over, eighty-four pages
of advertisements were to be ploughed through before the
stories started, and the highly popular journal enjoyed a
vast circulation.

Only the first two photographs were used, although the

other three would be in the hands of Houghton Smith, the editor, ready for use in the second article to come out in March of the next year. He would already have had assurances from top experts in psychic photography that the photographs were genuine; in any case, controversy, that great seller of magazines, would certainly flare up.

On the front cover appears for the first time a phrase which was to haunt literature on the Cottingley Fairies for years: 'AN EPOCH MAKING EVENT ... DESCRIBED BY A. CONAN DOYLE.' The photograph of Elsie and the gnome, taken in September 1917, faced the opening page. The caption ran thus:

IRIS AND THE DANCING GNOME

[An untouched enlargement from the original negative.]
THIS PICTURE AND THE EVEN MORE EXTRAORDINARY ONE OF THE FAIRIES ON PAGE 465 ARE THE TWO MOST ASTOUNDING PHOTOGRAPHS EVER PUBLISHED. HOW THEY WERE TAKEN IS FULLY DESCRIBED IN SIR A. CONAN DOYLE'S AMAZING ARTICLE (See Page 466)

It is unlikely that Doyle had much to do with the choice of a first photograph to go alongside this article, and likely that the caption stemmed from the editorial enthusiasm of a member of the *Strand* staff.

The early words of the article are in sharp contrast to the dramatic prose under the caption. Further, Doyle's verdict on whether the matter is proven or not is made clear in the first photograph, which begins:

Should the incidents here narrated, and the photographs

attached, hold their own against the criticism which they will excite, it is no exaggeration to say that they will mark an epoch in human thought. I put them and all the evidence before the public for examination and judgement. If I am myself asked whether I consider the case to be absolutely and finally proved, I should answer that in order to remove the last faint shadow of doubt I should wish to see the result repeated before a disinterested witness.

Doyle had written the article before his departure for Australia and did not hear about the last three photographs until he was in Melbourne, towards the end of 1920. Hence his opinion here is based upon the first two; when the other three came along, he eventually decided to commit himself and write his book on the subject, entitled, *The Coming of the Fairies*, which was completed in the winter of 1921 and published in March 1922.

He outlined how he came to hear of the photographs from Felicia Scratcherd and testifies as to the character and standing of Gardner. ('Who has ever been my most efficient collaborator, to whom all credit is due. Mr Gardner, it may be remarked, is a member of the Executive Committee of the Theosophical Society, and a well-known lecturer on occult subjects.') Doyle had known Sinnett, a prominent founder member of the society thirty years before, but had tended to keep the organization at a distance, for he preferred to pursue his research and missionary work alone. He was often in dispute with the Society for Psychical Research, and resigned in the 1920s over the authenticity of data from the Castle Millesimo in Italy, where sittings had been conducted by Professor Bozzano and from which remarkable reports had come forth. Doyle, typically perhaps, believed the phenomena that others doubted. For those wishing to pursue such a matter, the works of Bozzano and Gwendoline Hack are lengthy and detailed accounts, no fraud was ever discovered, and the reputation of Bozzano, in particular, escalated in the 1930s. His book *Discarnate Influence in Human Life* has become a classic work and is much sought after.

However, support for the luminous Bozzano did not extend to objectivity in the case of the fairy photographs. Although he had begun his article cautiously enough, Doyle was soon providing his critics with deadly ammunition in terms of being overbiased in favour of the dancing figures around Frances being from the fairy kingdom. Although he made use of an item massively associated with Sherlock Holmes, his imaginative prose was more associated with the romantic in him than the sleuth streak: 'I will now make a few comments upon the two pictures, which I have studied long and earnestly with a high-power lens . . . there is an ornamental rim to the pipe of the elves which shows that the graces of art are not unknown among them. And what joy in their complete abandon of their little graceful figures as they let themselves go in the dance! They may have their shadows and trials as we have, but at least there is a great gladness manifest in the demonstration of their life.'

It is clear from the above that Doyle had come to believe in the genuineness of the first photograph. A further examination of the print led him to a deduction concerning a gravitational process: '. . . the two upheld hands of the elves seen under a high-power lens do not appear to be human, nor does the left foot of the figure capering upon the right. The hands seem furred at the edges and the fingers to be in a solid mass . . . It is notable that one figure which is without wings is the one which is sinking into herbage . . .'

Such an apparent descent may, or may not, have been associated with lack of wing power, of course. Yet Doyle is doing no more than most of us in our day-to-day lives: we perceive a situation, locate it within our experience and (perhaps unconsciously) look for clues to support our judgement. If we see a picture of Arthur Scargill, it is our immediate perception from our past experiences of hearing about him that counts; the same could be said for Mrs Thatcher. Thus our gallant knight decided that the figures were not of human origin, and made inferences accordingly, right or wrong.

Right from the very first letters to Arthur Wright, both Gardner and Doyle had emphasized that the story would probably cause a stir, since the *Strand* was very popular and enjoyed a wide circulation. It was decided to use aliases: Elsie became Iris and Frances Alice, and they were of the Carpenter family in Dalesby, referred to by Gardner as 'a quaint old-world village in Yorkshire'. As has been pointed out in the first chapter, its inhabitants had been convincingly urbanized by hard industrial times, and there is no mention by E.L.G. of the town hall or Mechanics Institute, nor of the mill at which worked many of the sleepy villagers.

Doyle, in particular, entreated Elsie's father to keep quiet about the whole affair. He foresaw that 'a hundred charabancs' might descend on Cottingley following the publication of the news of the fairies. In the early part of his article he justifies the use of aliases: 'Mr Gardner tells his own story presently, so I will simply say that at that period he got into direct and friendly touch with the Carpenter family. We are compelled to use such a pseudonym and to withold the exact address, for it is clear that their lives would be much more interrupted by correspondence and callers if their identity were too clearly indicated.'

Rarely has such a scheme failed so quickly and so miserably. Within a week of the article being published, the *Daily Herald* had a reporter up at Cottingley, interviewing Polly, the subterfuge having been swiftly discovered.

It is popularly supposed that it was a reporter from the *Westminster Gazette* who went to Yorkshire and made enquiries which resulted in finding the true names of the Carpenter family. In fact, the *Herald* man was there weeks before, and I have heard it said that a letter was sent to London by some illwisher. It is unlikely that the matter will ever be settled. (If, like me, you were born and bred in the West Riding, you will appreciate the odd mixtures of guile, humour and treachery which are intermixed in our otherwise worthy and outspoken natures.)

The influence of Edward Gardner is heavily stamped over the 3,000 words of Doyle's first article, about a third of which is taken up by the Theosophist's report. In best scientific fashion, he systematically reports the technical details surrounding the first two photographs as follows:

Camera used:	'The Midg quarter plate'
Plates:	Imperial Rapid
Fairies photo:	July 1917. Day brilliantly hot and sunny. About 3 p.m. Distance: 4 feet. Time: 1/50th second exposure.
Gnome photo:	September 1917. Day bright, but not as above. About 4 o'clock. Distance 8 feet. Time 1/50th second.

Alas, for reasons outlined elsewhere in the book, the prints displayed are retouched originals and, of course, E.L.G. gives no details at all as to who improved the original sepia (rather blurred) prints from Arthur Wright's camera. In retrospect, of course, it is astounding that nobody challenged the prints outright and gave some professionally based opinion that, bearing in mind the composition of the setting and figures, some sort of specialist attention must have been given.

But in the article there is a snap of Gardner (soulful, bearded, bow-tied and backgrounded by the waterfall), and the caption reads: 'Mr E. L. Gardner standing behind the bank on which Alice is seen leaning in the photograph below.'

On the same page Elsie has been photographed, clad in the fashionable clothes of the day, a deadpan nineteen-year-old, as she obligingly leans, with the caption: 'Alice leaning on the bank on which the fairies were dancing, as shown in the photograph on page 465.'

To our perceptions, jaded as they are by interminable analyses on the media as to the selection and presentation of news (from the Falklands Crisis via Greenham Common to the Hitler Diaries from the East German hayloft), this may seem rather crude propaganda indeed. The reference to 'a high power lens' by Doyle, the preciseness of Gardner's prose, the shutter speed, the photographs of the actual spots where the supposed spirits had been seen – such details were calculated to move 1920 *Strand* readers towards an acceptance of the veracity of the prints. Gardner is adamant in his belief: 'Extraordinary and amazing as these photographs may appear, I am now quite convinced of their entire genuineness, as indeed would everyone else be who had the same evidence of transparent honesty and simplicity that I had.'

It was unlike Doyle to use another's prose so substantially in one of his articles. He was a strong individualist and preferred putting forward his own views based on his personal opinions or deductions from data which he himself had collected. Some would see it as strangely coincidental that he happened to be in the rushed state of preparing for an arduous Australian tour and had to sail in August, so that he could not be in Britain when the article appeared, and neither had he time to verify any details for himself. Thus, in view of the strong demand from the magazine for a Christmas article, he had no option but to rely on Gardner.

His principal reason for interesting himself in the bizarre case appears in the last paragraph of his article: 'The recognition of their existence will jolt the material twentieth-century mind out of its heavy ruts in the mud, and will make it admit that there is a glamour and mystery to life. Having discovered this, the world will not find it so difficult to accept that spiritual message supported by physical facts which has already been so convincingly put before it.'

But the habits of thought and existing belief systems sixty years ago, as now, have been shown to be of paramount importance when there is exposure to new ideas. We read and perceive to reinforce our comfortable opinions, and Doyle's assessment of the evidence for both fairy life and spiritualism was over-optimistic when he wrote his article in 1920. Today, perhaps, there is a more liberal tolerance of psychic phenomena, but the whole area of the occult is complex and nebulous. As agnostics may say, it is very difficult to believe that there is anything in it, and it is just as difficult to believe that there is nothing in it.

Doyle's first Christmas article still casts shadows and raises questions sixty years later. What of the length of Elsie's hand in the gnome photograph? Was it 'camera slant', as Frances suggests? And what of the other psychic experiences of the girls? Why did Elsie persistently draw fairies from twelve or so onwards, as described by those at school with her?

And what of others who have seen fairies?

Doyle's second article appeared in the *Strand* some three months after the first 'epoch-making' Christmas number contribution and is much more characteristic of the author's general style. It contains no verbatim reports from others, and is much longer – some 6,000 words, about twice the length of the earlier piece.

It is headed thus:

EVIDENCE FOR FAIRIES
BY
A. CONAN DOYLE
WITH MORE FAIRY PHOTOGRAPHS

This article was written by Sir A. Conan Doyle before actual photographs of fairies were known to exist. His departure for Australia prevented him from revising the article in the new light which has so strikingly strengthened his case. We are glad to be able to set before our readers two new fairy photographs, taken by the same girls, but of more recent date than those which created so much discussion when they were published in our Christmas number, and of even greater interest and importance. They speak for themselves.

The article is illustrated by the Leaping Fairy photograph and Elsie offering harebells to another figure. It will be seen from the captions beneath the fairy pictures that the *Strand's* public stance was to accept the supposed genuineness of the snaps, and such phrases as 'hovering for a moment' and 'standing almost still' would certainly sway some marginal readers, hardly able to believe, into accepting that the prints showed what they purported – real fairies.

The prose of Doyle is driving and lucid. He begins with the stance of sceptics when faced by hitherto unreported phenomena – as in the case of, say, amphibious creatures. Those who have seen accept, while those who have not doubt. As Doyle writes of such circumstances, 'The sceptics would hold the field.'

He then moves into what must become a most fashionable area of thought, if parapsychology is to move forward more in the next hundred years than the last – that of theory in psychic matters. He refers to the seventy years of spiritualist data which had accumulated and from which tentative hypotheses might emerge: one being the dividing line between the physical and paraphysical, in terms of energy vibrations and matter. This is an old and rather vague theme to grasp, but parallels with elements interchanging (fire to air, or air to water in the form of clouds) give some sort of imaginative lead. Transformation and change are salient features of all forms of life, and to confine such processes to the material alone may be overcautious when faced with novel or inexplicable observations. Unusual happenings or appearances may call for unusual reasoning, notably at the levels of concepts, theories and hypotheses, to direct research.

Doyle draws tellingly on evidence and quotes generously on credible accounts, but perhaps the most arresting is from his own family. He had three children in his second, and very happy, marriage, and the posed picture in this book is one taken in the mid-twenties, when Doyle was on his world travels and took his wife and young daughter with him. Jean, the bespectacled little girl, twists away from the camera by chance. When I recently sent her a copy of this snap, she commented how awful it was to wear glasses and what a blessing it was that they had not been shown. This formidable daughter of Doyle, now Lady Bromet, went on to become a senior officer in the WAAF and is a spirited and vocal champion of her father today. 'He left matters to others,' she once remarked to me. 'He put his trust in so-called experts. He was more concerned at the time with organizing his trip to Australia.'

A personal experience is given in the article. 'My younger family consists of two little boys and one small girl, very truthful children, each of whom tells with detail the exact circumstances and appearance of the creature. To each it happened only once, and in each case it was a single little figure, twice in the garden, once in the nursery.'

Mention is made of many other instances where children have seen fairies, and I have found at least half a dozen who have done so in my enquiries over the past few years. In the last chapter of this book, I deal with other cases, in addition to the dozen or so given by Doyle in his second *Strand* article.

Doyle quotes Baring Gould, Violet Tweedale, Tom Tyrell, Tom Charman and the experiences of two solemn contemporaries, Mr Turvey and Mr Lonsdale. As often, Doyle is at pains to assure the reader that no frivolity of character is creeping in anywhere when he gives a brief description of the latter. 'Knowing Mr Lonsdale as I do to be a responsible, well-balanced and honourable man, I find such evidence as this very hard to put on one side.'

The account of the gentlemen seeing fairies, bringing as it does a whiff of stable, class-ridden Edwardian England, verges irresistibly on the comic. It bears quoting at some length:

Mr Lonsdale, of Bournemouth, is also a well known sensitive. The latter has given me the following account of an incident which he observed some years ago in the presence of Mr Turvey.

'I was sitting', says Mr Lonsdale, 'in his company in his garden at Branksome Park. We sat in a hut which had an open front looking on to the lawn. We had been perfectly quiet for some time, neither talking nor moving, as was often our habit. Suddenly I was conscious of a movement on the edge of the lawn, which on that side went up to a grove of pine trees. Looking closely, I saw several little figures dressed in brown peering through the bushes. They remained quiet for a few minutes then disappeared. In a few seconds a dozen or more small people about two feet in height, in bright clothes and with radiant faces, ran on to the lawn dancing hither and thither. I glanced at Turvey to see if he saw anything, and whispered 'Do you see them?' He nodded. The fairies played about, gradually approaching the hut. One little fellow, bolder than the others, came to a croquet hoop close to the hut and, using the hoop as a horizontal bar, turned round and round on it, much to our amusement. Some of the others watched him, while others danced about, not in any set dance, but seemingly moving in sheer joy. This continued for four or five minutes, when suddenly, evidently in response to some signal or warning from those dressed in brown, who had remained at the end of the lawn, they all ran into the wood. Just then a maid appeared coming from the house with tea. Never was tea so unwelcome, as evidently its appearance was the cause of the disappearance of our little visitors.'

Reactions to this seemingly sincere account will vary. Some will imagine that the friends were hallucinating, perhaps physically influenced by the drowsy summer afternoon. It is hard to image that the testimony has been fabricated, but there is always the possibility of successive reportings being embellished. A general reaction, consonant with the adult public attitude towards fairies ('A rational person doesn't believe in fairies,' remarked the effervescent Labour MP Austin Mitchell to me on one occasion), is that the story must be false somewhere. After all, millions of people sit out on lawns during the summer, and none see fairies – therefore such a strikingly unusual account taxes the tolerance of most.

Yet Doyle endorses the validity of this account and goes on to give eye-witness fairy-sightings from those mentioned earlier. True to the logic of detection, he looks for common features – or disparities – in the descriptions. The appearances of fairies and elves are thus given:

Baring Gould:	Small green man fifteen inches high.
Violet Tweedale:	Tiny green man, five inches long, swinging on a leaf.
Mrs H. of Sussex:	Little creature, half a foot high, dressed in leaves.
Tom Tyrell:	Pixies – about twelve or fifteen inches high.
Tom Charman:	The creatures are of many sizes from a few inches to several feet.

The similarities in appearance of pixies, fairies and elves run true to illustrations in children's books, and again critics will shake their heads and maintain that imagination follows on from expectations: if one is brought up in childhood to associate nature sprites with rural settings and conventional fairy clothing, any such delusions will have such features. All I would say, from having spoken to perhaps a dozen people, young and old, who have seen gnomes or fairies, is that I was impressed by their frank, matter-of-fact and open manner. The most lengthy and detailed descriptions of fairy life were, of course, given to me by Frances.

Doyle, after giving several lengthy accounts from those who have experienced fairies, concludes his article on a speculative note under the hearing 'What *are* these creatures?' He quotes David Gow, editor of the influential spiritualist publication *Light*, as saying that the creatures are 'really life forms which have developed along some separate line of evolution, and which for some morphological reason have assumed human shape in the strange way in which Nature reproduces her types like the figures on the mandrake root or the frost ferns on the window'.

An interesting explanation is also quoted from Farnese, author of *A Wanderer in the Spirit Lands*, published in 1896. He maintains that elementals are a lower form of life and that, as nations advance and grow more spiritual, 'These lower forms die out from the astral plane of the earth's sphere.' This links, interestingly, with some schools of thought which maintain that non-industrial nations, such as those inhabiting Ancient Egypt, Greece and Rome, experienced such forms as the faun, dryad and naiad, all of which are now no longer seen. Yet others may deny that we have grown more spiritual but that the driving materialism of our age has caused these 'lower forms', often associated with rural settings, to die out.

Doyle ended his article on a note of utility: 'One may well ask what connection has this fairy-lore with the essays upon the fate of the human soul which have formed this series. The connection is slight and indirect, consisting only in the fact that anything which widens our conceptions of the possible, and shakes us out of our time-rutted lines of thought, helps to regain our elasticity of mind and thus be more open to new philosophies.'

Alas, our worthy writer, like many who had not studied effects of media communications, under-estimated the power of thought habits to persist in the face of new ideas, especially in the case of conceptions of the possible. Our belief systems, underpinned by emotionally held ideologies built up slowly down the years, not only resist radical change but also tend to tailor any new data to fit in with existing personal knowledge structures. Such phrases as 'it's only common sense' or 'it's only natural' or 'everybody knows that' are often used to sustain what is felt to be the truth of matters. It is no accident that television transmissions have come to be related more to what viewers believe in than to the content of the message and the 'hypodermic' effect which many supposed would prevail in the earlier days of the medium.

'It is at the lowest an interesting speculation which gives an added charm to the silence of the woods and the wilderness of the moorland' are the concluding words of Conan Doyle's second article, which he reproduced in full in his book *The Coming of the Fairies* in 1922. Indeed, a large section of that fairly short book is taken up by material printed in the two *Strand* articles, and it also includes a full account from the medium Geoffrey

Hodson, who was sent to Cottingley in August 1921 in order to verify the girls' story and, if possible, take some more photographs.

But it is to the reactions of reviewers of these articles, published in December 1920 and March 1921, that we might next turn.

8

Critics and Champions

*'Such absurd ideas will result in later life in manifes-
tations of nervous disorder and mental disturbances.'*
Major Hall-Edwards. Radium medical expert

The two articles published by Doyle in December 1920
and March 1921 provoked a considerable flurry of
press comment.

The general reaction was not only of doubt but also of
curiosity and wonder. The author was highly respected
and the Theosophical Society, although not the force it
had been, still commanded solid respect and Gardner was
not only president of the London Blavatsky Lodge but
also the chief officer responsible for any photography
and lantern slides. Further, interest in the occult was
keen, and both Doyle and Gardner felt that they were
living in times when beliefs in some presiding and just
Outer World might shift in their favour. Critics were thus
cautious in their reactions.

The editorial of the *Manchester City News* summed up the attitudes of many in its issue of 29 January 1921: 'It seems to us at this point that we must either believe in the almost incredible mystery of the fairy, or in the almost incredible wonder of faked photographs. Which is it to be? Perhaps when Mr Gardner comes to Manchester he will settle our doubts. His lecture will certainly be worth hearing and his lantern slides worth seeing.'

Maurice Hewlett, an influential poet and essayist of the time, made a similar point, though modifying his presentation to reflect his own opinion. 'It is easier to believe in faked photographs than fairies,' he wrote in *John o'London's* weekly.

A scrutiny of the carefully kept files of cuttings of reviewers in the Brotherton Collection at Leeds University gives a somewhat broader spectrum, including the reactions of critics. The attack against those who would fake fairy photographs was led, appropriately enough, by a military man. He was one Major Hall-Edwards, also a radium expert, and he had no doubt as to the falsity of the snaps. Furthermore, he was also concerned with the dangers of the young entering into such occult realms, and his vigorous article in the *Birmingham Post* included the following sharp grapeshot: 'On the evidence I have no hesitation in saying that these photographs could have been "faked". I criticize the attitude of those who declared there is something supernatural in the circumstances attending the taking of these pictures because, as a medical man, I believe that the inculcation of such absurd ideas into the minds of children will result in later life in manifestations of nervous disorder and mental disturbances.'

Such effects were notably absent from the lives of Elsie

and Frances, for both exhibited unusual physical vigour and mental strength in the prime of their lives. Elsie served in a voluntary corps, as an officer, in India during the 1940s and was active concerning the rehabilitation of Japanese prisoners of war. Frances, for years, was a very efficient medical secretary who could take down shorthand in excess of 150 words a minute, notably when recording reports from doctors literally crimson from their operations in the surgery. The children of both have also been conspicuously successful: Elsie's son, Glenn, was a champion rower and is now a prominent executive and Conservative councillor; Kit, the daughter of Frances, married a professor, and her son David played a conspicuous part in the design of the Barbican in London. Such flourishings of offspring could not have taken place in households where mothers suffered 'nervous disorders and mental disturbances'.

But the irate major was probably putting into words something that was felt by many. Any excursions into the realms of fairies, witches and spirits have links with black magic and all the gory trappings of horror films, to say nothing of countless radio and telly plays where luckless individuals go mad or are found in the morning with hair white and their dead gaze staring out in horror.

So it is that 'Don't be silly!' and 'It's best not to tamper with the unknown' have general acceptance, rather than any open-minded attitudes of enquiry. Thus the rich fantasies of children are often squashed, and social attitudes of 'being down to earth' are subtly inculcated.

But in the winter of 1921 there were still reviewers prepared to give Tinkerbell an even chance of existence. Consider the two following sensitive comments:

South Wales Argus: The day we kill Santa Claus with our statistics and our photographs we shall have plunged a glorious world into deepest darkness.

The Day's Thought: 'Tis as true as the fairy tales told in books.'

The Sun, USA (on Doyle and the photographs): But he does not bring the fairies nearer to us. The soul of the fairy is its evanescence. Its charm is the eternal doubt, rose-tinted with the shadow of a hope. But the thrill is all in ourselves.

It was left to a magazine, appropriately enough entitled *Truth*, to make what was probably the pithiest comment: 'For the true explanation of the fairy photographs what is wanted is not a knowledge of occult phenomena but a knowledge of children.'

There are many accounts of children having seen fairies, as I am fairly sure that Frances did. Also, in my opinion, I would think that we are only at the very beginning of fairy investigations at Cottingley, as the last chapter in my book suggests. And of crucial importance is the need to sympathize with children and, above all perhaps, to listen to them.

Two strong supporters of the girls and the authenticity of the photographs were the educationist Margaret McMillan and the novelist de Vere Stacpoole.

Margaret McMillan first. She had pioneered the education and better health of slum children in Bradford and had been awarded the CBE in 1917. She was a member of the Independent Labour Party, an organization hardly noted for its interest in fairies. She was also an ex-actress and an heiress who could have lived comfortably in London rather than come north to ease the plight of poverty-stricken children. She had an arresting platform speaking-manner and much experience in dealing with all classes of adults and children. Her enthusiastic endorsement of the photos thus links more with her basic Scots mysticism than her Socialist rationalism: 'How wonderful to these dear children such a wonderful gift has been vouchsafed,' she wrote to Gardner. She had forsaken a plush life for that of a social reformer, so that her experience of people had been wide in her fifty years and she was by no means a starry-eyed sentimentalist. (Shaw referred to her as 'a cantankerous old woman'.)

De Vere Stacpoole had been a doctor attracted to literature by reading Carlyle, and his adventure stories are well known. He was a Celt like Margaret McMillan, she being a Scot and he Irish. These words, taken from a letter he wrote to Gardner, might be taken as monumental evidence that character may not be easily discerned from a photograph:

> Look at Alice's face
> Look at Iris's face
> There is an extraordinary thing called TRUTH which has ten million faces and forms – it is God's currency and the cleverest coiner or forger can't imitate it.

This hopeful comment, however, is open to debate. One has only to consider such a programme as *Call My Bluff* to view how easily the sophisticated can simulate truth, and most of us learn to lie fairly convincingly from early childhood on, or at least to make truth to suit the occasion.

The opinions of expert photographers varied somewhat.

In early 1920 Kodak declared that, 'The fairies couldn't be true . . . the photographs must have been faked somehow.' In a letter to Gardner they put forward the idea that expensive equipment might have been used, including a studio set-up. In fact, as can be seen from a comparison between one of Arthur Wright's original prints and the picture appearing in the *Strand* article, it is obvious that Gardner and his associates *had* retouched the original. (Yet their sin, it could be argued, is no worse than any photographer of popstars or, indeed, family portraits, where we are often presented at our best.)

They made two points:

a) The negatives are single exposure, and the plates show no signs of being faked work; but that cannot be taken as conclusive evidence for their genuineness.

b) The photographs might have been made by using the glen features and the girl as a background; then enlarging the prints from these and painting in the figures; then taking half-plate and finally quarter-plate snaps, suitably lighted. All this would be clever work and take time.

A minor mystery now presents itself, concerning Harold Snelling, the photographic expert called in by Gardner who examined the glass plate negatives which had been sent to Gardner in London by Arthur Wright. The crucial part of his report ran thus:

Re: Two Fairy Photographs

These two negatives are entirely genuine and unfaked photographs of single exposure, open air work, show movement in all fairy figures, and there is no trace whatever of studio work involving card or paper models, dark backgrounds, painted figures etc. In my opinion they are both straight, untouched figures.

Harold Snelling.

It is likely that Snelling wrote in good faith, but how is it possible for even an experienced photographer to be certain of movement in figures? The original sepia reproduction was blurred, perhaps caused by the developing chemicals or light variations within the enclosed and high banks of the beck.

But in spite of the glowing references described by Gardner to Doyle ('What Snelling doesn't know about faked photographs isn't worth knowing'), Leslie Gardner, his son, wrote an article for the Folklore Society in 1973 which suggests that some might not accept the testimony: 'For almost certainly Snelling would have been considered mad. He was an untidy little man with unruly hair and large staring eyes and his fingers were habitually stained with photographic chemicals.'

So it was that opinion on the two articles was mixed but tended to be critical. Especially there was a feeling that some sort of follow-up, in terms of other photographs and interviews, was needed – and this Edward Gardner next attempted, endorsed by his famous ally, who felt that a greater concentration of photographic and mediumistic expertise might verify matters.

9

The 1921 Expedition

Austin Mitchell: *But that indicates that both of you were practical jokers.*
Frances: *We were.*

Television interview, September 1976

The year 1921 dawned briskly for E. L. Gardner. He had obtained five photographs from the girls, and there seemed to be prospects of getting more. The great Doyle had written from Australia expressing appreciation and hinting that there would be a book out on it all before long, to be written by himself and E.L.G. It would sell at 5 shillings and would be called *The Fairies – their modern rediscovery*, or some similar title based on the facts of the case from Doyle's articles in the *Strand*, and Gardner was to be given an opportunity to express his Theosophical views.

In February Gardner had written to Polly saying that the book would be out in April, and he was also making arrangements for a cinematograph camera to be sent to Cottingley, so that the girls might get used to working it.

But matters slowed down. The book was deferred, for Doyle's agent was doubtful about two names on the cover in relation to possible sales. The cine-camera was not despatched, but Doyle arranged for Geoffrey Hodson, a medium in his thirties at the time, to journey north in August and sit with the girls and perhaps increase the strength of the surrounding auric field so that even stronger shapes might materialize.

A rather cryptic copy of a letter sent to Doyle by E.L.G. expresses the former's reluctance to meet for any further discussions:

> April 15th 1921.
> My Dear Doyle,
>   Your note to hand I quite understand. Just let me know when you have the spare time and I will meet you. There is no immediate hurry as I explained.

Thus in August Frances came over from Scarborough yet again, and the man from the Theosophical Society, bow-tied and earnest as ever, left cameras and plates and instructions.

There is a record of Gardner's field notes for the first part of the expedition, scrawled in pencil on the notepaper of the Midland Hotel, Bradford, where he stayed for the first few days. His notes are now in the Brotherton Collection and I reproduce them exactly as he wrote them:

> Tuesday Aug. 2nd [1921]. Arrived 1 pm. Showery. Rained heavily in afternoon. Frances at Cottingley. Elsie home in eve.

Wednesday – Aug. 3rd. Cottingley 11.00 for most part fine. Glen after 2 o.c. Scouts camp! Walked the glen. Elsie remarked on a different 'feeling'. Left girls alone. At willow for an hour. Nothing 'happened'. Walked into woods about three miles. 'No good'. Home about 5 o.c.

Thursday Aug. 4th. Cool, windy, fine and dull. Cottingley 2.30 Girls had gone up beck. Camp gone. Followed and 'spied' – then met 'nothing doing' – left them to continue – girls came in about 5 p.m. No results. Wet evening.

Friday Aug. 5th.
Rained all day continuously (Pictures in evening).

Saturday Aug. 6th. Very windy. Fine except two showers. Cottingley 1 pm. Girls up beck at 10 am. – Waited and they came home 1.30 'saw nothing'. Left to meet Hodson. Arranged not to call till Monday.

Sunday (dull and rainy) Nothing.

Monday Aug. 8. sunny intervals. Showery, high wind. Mr & Mrs Hodson. Up beck from 11.30 to 4.30. Power felt. Nothing seen.

Tuesday. Mr & Mrs Hodson & girls up beck from 12 o.c. Fairly fine but overcast and windy. Nothing seen.

Wed. Aug. 10th. Raining heavily all morning. All met at about 2.30. Up beck 3 to 6. Very heavy and lowering. Many n. spirits seen by girls & H. No photography.

Thurs. Aug. 11th. Raining heavily all day. Arranged for H to try each day till Fri. 19th.
I came home in storms of rain.

Now these jottings, at first sight heavily weighted in favour of the meteorological, begin to cast a few shadows on the case of the Cottingley Fairies. Why did E.L.G. 'spy' on the girls? What did he hope to see? Why is there merely a brief reference to 'Many n. spirits' seen on Wednesday 10 August when one might have expected considerably more detail? If E.L.G. records the weather so closely, how is it that there are but two words (and one abbreviated at that!) regarding the most important part of his whole observations? Such shortcomings in research commentaries extend elsewhere.

In both *The Coming of the Fairies* by Doyle in 1922 and *A Book of Real Fairies* by Gardner in 1947, a generous part of the text is taken up by Hodson's account of nature spirits seen at Cottingley in August 1921. In the case of E.L.G.'s book, it is some eight sides out of a total of fifty-three, and in Doyle's volume fifteen sides out of 194. It is of interest that Gardner quotes Hodson's notes as 'being supplied to Sir Arthur Conan Doyle'. Doyle persists with his pseudonyms in the 1922 book (why Hodson should require protecting is hardly clear) and refers to him as a friend 'whom I will call Mr Serjeant, who held a commission in the Tank Corps in the war, and is an honourable gentleman with neither the will to deceive nor any conceivable object in doing so'.

As has been seen, the period 5–11 August was rainy and unproductive. By contrast, according to the notes made by Hodson and passed to Doyle, the period from 12–18 August positively reverberated with 'n. spirits' of all kinds, coming from all directions. Nude water nymphs sported in the beck, water fairies appeared at the waterfall, wood elves raced over fallen beeches, brownies, elves and gnomes danced in the moonlight, and a fairy band arrived

in a field supervised by a fairy director. On the 18th
a Golden Fairy appears and has an appreciable effect
upon the clairvoyant: 'She has cast a fairy spell over
me completely subjugating the mental principle – leaves
me staring wild-eyed in amongst the leaves and flowers.'
Hodson's notes then are as pregnant with elementals and
incidents as Gardner's are barren.

From this emerges our darkest shadow, in the form of
the question: Why was it that neither Elsie and Frances
nor Hodson made use of a camera to try to photograph
this rich miscellany of elemental life?

The only comment I had from Elsie and Frances was
that they didn't bother with cameras. Perhaps the clue
to the matter is Hodson's comment on the Golden Fairy
which sent him wild-eyed among the leaves and flowers:
'She is not objectively visible on the physical plane.'

If, however, reference is made to the telecast by YTV in
September 1976, we have the following shattering dialogue
between Austin Mitchell and the ladies – all very spontaneous and sincere sounding, with no 'ers' or pauses:

A.M.:	You came down here with a Mr Hodson, a medium …
Frances:	That's right.
A.M.:	You told him you saw fairies. Were you pulling his leg or not?
Frances:	No. We saw them.
Elsie:	We saw them.

(Sustained and sudden laughter from both Elsie and
Frances.)

Frances:	Well, he was a phoney, we knew he was …
Elsie:	Yes.
Frances:	We set off straightforward and we were told if we saw anything to say … and we did … and

we'd say can you see that over by the willow
tree and Elsie would look and say yes ... and
then it would get bigger and bigger and Elsie
would add a bit and I'd add a bit ... and
eventually we said we saw lots of things and
we never saw fairies again after that ... we
were ... we got so that we saw fairies chained
to oak trees – we saw all sorts of things ...

A.M.: But that indicates that you're both practical
jokers.

Frances: We were.

Elsie Yes.

All of which contrasts rather sadly with the rigidity of
Conan Doyle's account: 'Seated with the girls, he saw
all that they saw, and more, for his powers proved to
be considerably greater. Having distinguished a psychic
object, he would point in the direction and ask them for
a description, which he always obtained correctly within
the limit of their powers ...'

So it is that the 1921 data are inconclusive. Both Elsie
and Frances said that they saw elementals, and it is doubtful indeed if the rich and varied accounts of fairy life given
by Hodson are entirely fictitious.

Consider the following: 'Elsie sees a flight of little
mannikins, imp-like in appearance, descending slantwise
on to the grass. They form into two lines which cross each
other as they come down. One line is coming vertically
down, feet touching head, the other comes across them
shoulder to shoulder. On reaching the ground they all
run off in different directions, all serious, as if intent upon
some business.'

I find it hard to accept that such words are fiction from
Hodson's imagination, designed to deceive for money

made from a book. Hodson's lapses in agreeing with fictitious figures described by the girls are lamentable but in keeping with patterns of behaviour of other mediums. Often such folk, when genuine psychic phenomena do not come along when expected, will slip into prevarication or lies. The whole area of mediumship is shot through with fraud and truth alike – sometimes the fraud is unconscious, but it seems plain that Hodson strikes a sincere note with some of his data.

Elsie would never talk much about Hodson or his accounts. She remembered him as something of a name-dropper; married to a lady rather older than himself and forever asking her such (to her falsely endearing) questions as 'Happy, darling?' and giving her a winning smile. She said that Hodson was more of a humorous salesman type, which is certainly at variance with the lofty seriousness of his later books.

In 1979, for instance, Hodson's *Music Forms* was published, the first edition having appeared in 1976. This is a colourfully illustrated quarto book in which 'superphysical effects of music' have been clairvoyantly observed by him. On the inside cover is an impressive photograph of an unusually good-looking man, immaculate about the collar and tie, and the wording runs: 'For some sixty years Mr Hodson has lectured for the Theosophical Society, speaking in America, England, Europe, South Africa, India, New Zealand, Australia and the Far East. He is also the author of about forty Theosophical and other books ... four times Director of Studies at the School of the Wisdom, at the International Headquarters of the Theosophical Society, in India.'

Many times I tried to elicit comments from Elsie and Frances on their extensive comments on Hodson's account of all the elemental life he saw with them around the beck. Both refused to read any of his books and considered him a fake.

'You'll just have to make up your own mind about it,' Elsie once told me, as I sat beside her, tape-recorder going and Doyle's book open at the page where Hodson writes, 'Elsie saw mannikins . . .' So I quietly buried the subject and picked up my ukelele, and Elsie, Frank and I rendered 'Margie' yet again, as Frank's home-made brew circulated. (I may not have dented Elsie's accounts, but it was good fun trying.)

I, personally, find it very difficult to believe that Hodson was the faker that Elsie and Frances declared him to be on the YTV programme. Doyle, generally a shrewd judge of people, chose him out of many, for several leading clairvoyants would have jumped at the chance of aiding him in his research in 1920. Hodson's lengthy accounts of angel life in such books as *The Coming of the Angels* and *The Science of Seership* are generally in the faintly irritating and nebulous prose of vague psychical research, but there is a certain purity of intention, a spiritual appreciation of other planes, a hope that mankind may one day be united cosmologically, the better to co-operate here on earth. If I had to pick one passage which suggests a worthy character writing from the heart, it would be this one from *The Science of Seership*. It concerns a tank in which he fought and a church he visited:

Tanks, like other instruments of warfare, express themselves largely by noise and movement. Inside the tank, the former characteristic is predominant, and outside, the latter. To those who have learned to love the silence, they are not the most desirable companions of daily toil; to live with them, to sleep in or under them, and to fight in them over a period of eighteen months is not the happiest occupation for a lover of peace ... that is our tank and we have lived with and fought in her for many months. Through her tiny loop-holes we have watched grim Death stalking by our side. We have heard his bullets rain like hail upon her flanks; we have driven her over deadly barbed wire entanglements, trenches and shell-holes. Heavy guns, deep sunken in the mud and despaired of by her crews, has she pulled out on to dry ground. She has brought back the wounded after many a show – and we would not willingly change her for another ...

At the end of one day he visited a little church in the valley of the Ternoise and describes his experience as he slumps into a seat at the end of a weary day of fighting in the tank:

Gradually there is a change. The altar appears outlined with white light, the sanctuary vibrant with power. My eyes are closed, but inner sight – deliberately inhibited for many years of War-time life – is aroused and aware. Behind and above the altar a form appears – tall and impassive – a man all red from head to foot, as if clad in crimson armour. He approaches and stands behind and a little above me. All fear gradually disappears, and a great joy wells up from within me. I feel, too, a sense of comradeship with him – as though he were my friend who gladly welcomes me in his church.

Dread of the near future has been with me. We are shortly going forward again, and are undertaking special training for a new departure in tank warfare. But now all fear leaves me: I feel supported, as though his armour were upon me and made me safe. A firm conviction comes that all will be well, that I shall not be alone in the Hell that has soon to be faced . . . that I shall come through!

Those, for me, are not the phrases of a poseur, a conman or one would make money from reporting fictitious psychic experiences.

Geoffrey Hodson died at the age of ninety-six in January 1983, in New Zealand. I had sent him a copy of my article in the December 1982 issue of the *Unexplained* which had come out a few weeks before, and I never knew whether he had read it or not.

As I mentioned previously, before he died I was fortunate enough to have associates Down Under who visited him with a tape-recorder. The somewhat sober interview came back all the way from New Zealand. A description label is carefully typed on the cassette: 'Mr G. Hodson answers questions relating to his personal experiences of the fairies in Cottingley Glen in 1921. 13 mins. each side. THE THEOSOPHICAL SOCIETY OF NEW ZEALAND.' It runs thus:

Voice: This is Frank Wilson of Birkenhead, New Zealand. I am very grateful for the opportunity of this short interview with Mr Geoffrey Hodson who has consented to answer some questions on the fairies. Mr Hodson, do you remember going to Cottingley in 1921 at the suggestion of Conan Doyle?

G.H.:   Yes, Mr Wilson, indeed I do, so extremely vivid were the experiences passed through whilst I was visiting the Cottingley Glen on several occasions . . . and with the two girls who took the photographs. Not only did I question them very closely concerning their experiences and photographs but I verified beyond question the complete straightforwardness of every answer they gave me. Perhaps most important in this connection was, and still is, the last photograph. It is the fifth and indistinct picture. Their answer to my question was that in their excitement at seeing the phenomena before them in the bunch of bluebells that they did not wait long enough but exposed the photograph rather before the materialization was complete.

[Hodson goes on to say that he considered Elsie and Frances clairvoyant.]

I would see fairies or gnomes coming near us but remain silent. Quite often, soon afterwards, one or other of the girls would exclaim 'There is a fairy!' and point to, or correctly describe, the creature. In my ninety-third year I am supervising the publication of the second edition of my book *The Kingdom of the Gods*.

Wilson: Do you think fairy life still exists in Cottingley?

G.H.: Yes indeed. I answer not from renewed research, for I have not revisited the place for a very large number of years. But members of the kingdom of fairies and angels exist and are active everywhere throughout nature. Furthermore, collaboration with certain orders of the angelic hosts in certain services can be very effective. Spiritual healing, for example. If I may say so, I advance these ideas and many others in parts four and five of my illustrated book *The Kingdom of the Gods*.

Wilson: In what form do fairies appear?

G.H.: A basic form is discernible in both fairies and angels. When a more objective self-expression is entered upon ... a process of more or less unconscious self-clothing in the matter of the

> ether and supra planes is instinctively carried
> out by the fairy people. This culminates in the
> temporary creation of an etheric body ensouled,
> interpenetrated and surrounded by the creator
> within. The reproduction is relatively fixed in
> form but built of continually flowing energies.
> All of which are arranged much as the usual
> pictures of fairies display.

So we came to the end of the first act of our drama. Doyle
received quite a lengthy and detailed report from Hodson,
giving a lavish account of his fairy sightings at Cottingley,
and his words were reproduced in Doyle's book and the
one brought out by Gardner in 1945.

Were his words true? Were they fiction? Is it possible
to say whether the fairies one person sees are truer than
those seen by others? Or untrue because others don't
see them?

Certainly the vast variety of nature spirits he claimed to
see were not photographed – the 1921 expedition was as
unsuccessful as the 1920 endeavours had been successful.

For four years, then, Elsie and Frances had sustained
their deceptions.

It was to be more than four decades later that the strange
affair was to surface once more.

Endings (1965–88)

❧ 10 ❧

The Case Revives

> *As for the photographs let's say they are pictures of figments of our imagination, Frances and mine, and leave it at that.*
>
> Elsie to a *Daily Express* reporter, May 1965

No more nature spirits were reported from Cottingley after 1921, and the publicity stemming from Doyle's subsequent book *The Coming of the Fairies* gradually died down, only modest sales being achieved.

Elsie left Yorkshire for America, when she met her future husband, Frank Hill, an engineer on leave from India. She moved back with him and led a pleasant life amidst servants, sunsets and a genial community of folk who, like Frank, were Scots. In consequence she picked up their accent, which she kept for the rest of her life. Her intonation down the years thus progressed from Bradfordian, Canadian to Scots, Frances having moved from South African via Cottingley tones to a Midlands accent. Such are significant oddities, some inner being tells me, although I know not why or wherefore.

Frances married a soldier, Sidney Way, who rose to the rank of Warrant Officer and had many postings at home and abroad, notably a long spell in Egypt. Her two children, Christine and David, have been unusually successful, as has Elsie's son Glenn. All three are happily married, with impressive children. Eventually Frances's husband left the Army, and the family settled in the Midlands.

Edward Gardner, after many lecture tours in Britain and one in America, rose in the ranks of the Theosophical Society and become one of its most prestigious members. In 1945, in his seventies, he brought out his book on the Cottingley Fairies, but he added little to Doyle's account. One might raise an eyebrow that he never called in such eminent psychical researchers as J. Arthur Hill of Thornton, Bradford, or the Rev. Charles Tweedale of Weston, near Otley. Both were friends of Doyle and could not only have helped with further research but perhaps raised interesting theoretical issues from their own experiences. After Hodson, no other sensitives were asked to visit Cottingley, supposedly teeming with nature spirits. This in itself is odd, in retrospect, but the affair became outmoded in the thirties.

However, Gardner's book is, or was, generally regarded as the standard work on the subject for many years and was reprinted several times. His book was entitled *Real Fairies* but contained little new, with the original report, Doyle's views and extensive reproductions from Hodson's perceptions being regurgitated. The veracity of the photos is stated to be almost undoubted – it is as if the actual passage of years had settled matters for him, as is often the case of histories written in benign retrospect.

Extracts from his work, a comparatively slender volume, were printed in the magazine *Prediction* dated October 1947. The magazine itself brings back something of those times, with its small 'utility' size and whiff of the fuel crisis and the austerity of the immediate post-war years. (In spite of the arrival of comparative affluence since then, occult presentations today are much the same at a popular level as in the 1940s.) The front cover itself suggested that our fairy story was securely located in an appropriately mysterious setting: a hooded lady peered into a crystal ball, with a looming genie of sorts in the background behind her, presumably at her service if required; and there were, all around, pyramids, scrolls, zodiac signs and, of course, a client whose palm our fortune-teller is touching, as she looks at a spread of cards and gazes hopefully into her crystal sphere.

Details of two leading articles in the magazine are prominently displayed on the cover. One is 'Horoscopes – Can they solve the Crisis?' by R. H. Naylor, whose horoscopes in 1939 failed to predict war; and the other is 'ELEMENTALS – AMAZING PICTURES – How Conan Doyle was convinced'. The latter piece, by Gardner, is subtitled 'ARE THEY GENUINE? – The full story of the Amazing Cottingley Photographs'. The photos of Elsie, her elongated hand and the gnome, and the one of Frances scrutinizing a fairy in mid-air are reproduced. A few phrases will serve to give the tone of the article:

The figures were declared to be made of no known fabric, to be homogeneous and to have moved ...

The weighing up of all the evidence, both of the

photographic testimony and the personal circumstances, enforced the conviction on Conan Doyle and myself that here was an epoch-making event that should be made widely known ...

The combination of simple clairvoyance, mediumship, youth and innocence with access to and a delight in the beauties of the glen were some of the exceptional circumstances that led to success.

It is easy at this point, with the hindsight of subsequent disclosures, to marvel at the apparent gullibility of Doyle and Gardner.

But they were little different from most of us. Habits of thought become entrenched; we tend to read what supports our belief systems, and we selectively perceive, favouring that which pleases or interests us, and ignore evidence or points of view which upset. (Festinger summarizes this with his elegant phrase 'cognitive dissonance' in the literature of psychology.)

By the mid-sixties it seemed that the affair had languished, perhaps forever. Elsie and her family had returned to Britain and bought a house in the Midlands, Frances and her demobilized husband lived on the South Coast, with her children grown up and away from home, and Polly had died in 1956 at seventy-nine, after being tenderly nursed by her daughter Elsie. ('Until she died,' Glenn Hill has said to me more than once, 'my grandmother knew nothing of the truth of the fairy photographs – she believed in them.')

It was about this time that I came across Gardner's book. I have been a student of parapsychology for most of my years, and I orientated towards the possibility of belief in the worth of the photographs almost at once. That they had been touched up was obvious. But what of the original prints? And the girls, sticking to the truth in the face of considerable pressure? I was strangely drawn to the whole odd affair.

My disposition has always been that of a spiritual optimist, for at nine, during a performance of *Peter Pan*, I actually stood up and cheered in the balcony when an endorsement of fairy life was called for to resuscitate a fading Tinkerbell, while more cautious believers clapped their hands. My hopeful nature was, however, tinged with regret that original prints and negatives would long since have been destroyed. I also remember regretting that the girls would probably be too aged now for anything approaching questioning at any level of significance (how wrong I was to be proved). Such information as I had amounted to rumours of the death of Frances in South Africa and several local stories involving Elsie's likely demise, and a variety of supposed accomplices, from tramps to slain World War I soldiers on leave.

But, quite suddenly, the first shivers of fairy resuscitation came in 1965, when a national daily decided to check on latest developments, having obtained Elsie's address in the Midlands from Yorkshire sources. Writing in the *Daily Express* in May, the enterprising reporter Peter Chambers described how he had tracked down Elsie (in her sixties) to 'a neat semi-detached house, with bay windows and a front garden and a family saloon visible in the garage'.

Chambers felt that there had been trickery of some kind, and Elsie, as in India, preferred that the matter should be buried and that people should make up their own minds. She was always concerned that it might lead people into the more unhealthy aspects of occult studies, particularly the less meaningful aspects of Spiritualism, with Ouija boards, amateur seances and all the rest of it. Many times did she tell me that she would rather people thought of her and Frances as 'a couple of solemn-faced comediennes' and disbelieved their story, rather than believe it and become over-involved in dubious dabblings with the unknown.

She therefore told Chambers that he would have to judge for himself, and she is quoted as saying, 'As for the photographs, let's say they are pictures of figments of our imagination, Frances and mine, and leave it at that.' So was born the assertion which she was to use time and time again in the 1970s, when being interviewed by various media men.

Chambers, however, plumped for something strange at the bottom of the garden and had ideas about cut-outs or painted figures – these being the popular ideas of how the snaps had been faked. Elsie thus succeeded in dampening journalistic influence, but only for a further six years.

After Edward Gardner's death in 1970, at a hundred, *Nationwide* revived the fairy story in a programme in early 1971. Lynn Lewis, an energetic, forceful producer, interviewed Elsie in her home and Frances at Epsom College, where she was matron. Lewis had been to Kodak and had heard expert opinion pronounce that the outline of the fairies was far too sharp for a Midg camera using a lens with an exposure of 1/50th of a second. One Kodak view was that dolls or models were used in the first two photographs, and some sort of double exposure in the last three. It was also suggested that the pictures had been devised by a person having a feeling for composition and that somebody other than the girls had perhaps been involved. A certain stylistic resemblance to photos taken by Elsie's father from her album and the five famous fairy photos was pointed out.

The programme opened with Lewis holding forth on the familiar story, with a background shot of the Theosophical home for the elderly where Edward Gardner had passed his last years, highly respected to the end and writing and lecturing almost up to his death. His memory had been championed by many, notably his son Leslie Gardner, who died in 1982. However, Lewis implied that money had been made for the Theosophical Society by Gardner's book and that, perhaps, it had helped with the maintenance of homes such as the one in which Gardner had died.

Shots were then shown of Elsie in her living-room, and she presented an amiable, if slightly uneasy figure. Then aged seventy, she was in excellent health and could still swim twenty lengths. Her replies were careful, and she paused often. Lewis must have thought that, indeed, she was on the edge of confessing all, but Elsie – as she was to do so often in the next few years – blandly turned aside any leading questions. The following dialogue comes from a tape made at the time.

Lewis: Now he [Gardner] is dead, can you speak up?
Elsie: I didn't want to upset Mr Gardner ... I don't mind talking now ...

Lewis then mentions that others think Elsie's father might have had a hand in the matter.

Elsie: I would swear on the Bible Father didn't know what was going on.
Lewis: Could you equally swear on the Bible that you didn't play any tricks?
Elsie: (after a pause) I took the photographs ... I took two of them ... no, three ... Frances took two ...
Lewis: Are they trick photographs? Could you swear on the Bible about that?

Elsie: (after a pause) I'd rather leave that open if you don't mind . . . but my father had nothing to do with it, I can promise you that . . .

Lewis: Have you had your fun with the world for forty years? Have you been kidding us for ten days?

Elsie laughs.

Elsie: (gently) I think we'll close it on that if you don't mind.

Frances once painted a vivid word-picture, as she so often did, of the approach made to her by the BBC for the programme: 'I knew as soon as I saw the BBC van who it was and what they wanted. It was outside the college, where I was matron, and my heart sank.'

So, once again, Frances was obliged firstly to find out what Elsie had said and secondly to state that she had nothing to add. For more than fifty years had she remained loyal to her promise and Elsie?

Lewis was, as with Elsie, forthright in his questioning:

Lewis: Did you have a crush on her?

Frances: (laughs) No. Not at all. She was young for her age. She used to play with my dolls.

But the general impression which came over was one of subterfuge, of something being hidden. But what? How had the photos been faked? What of those lost? Were there, as Frances said, fairies at Cottingley?

Such questions had a particular significance for the academics Katharine Briggs and Stewart Sanderson who happened to be watching the programme, for both had been students of fairy life most of their lives and were members of the Folklore Society.

It is to their reactions that we next turn.

11

The Frowns of the
Folklore Society

They must be fakes!
Stewart Sanderson to a *Daily Mail* reporter, early 1977

The long-established and prestigious Folklore Society does not obviously commit itself to a belief in fairies but rather to a close study of their recorded adventures. In this august body, for many years, the past histories of all manner of fairy folk, their traditional likes and dislikes, and their attitudes towards humans, have been sifted and detailed. The late Katharine Briggs, an eminent scholar and efficient bibliographer, recently produced a *Dictionary of Fairies*, and the few extracts below from the index will give some idea of the rigour and depth of her scholarship and research:

F 302.3.4.2. Fairies dance with youth till he goes insane.
KATE CRACKERNUTS.

F 316   Fairy lays curse on child. FAIRY GOD-
                 MOTHERS.
F 361.2.3:   Fairies bind man fast to ground after he has
                 attempted to capture fairy prince and prin-
                 cess. MISER ON THE FAIRY GUMP.
F 362:   Fairies cause diseases. BLIGHTS AND ILL-
                 NESSES ATTRIBUTED TO FAIRIES:
                 IMPETIGO.

There is a sombre warning to all of us who would probe further in the fairy world on p.152: 'These fairies evidently felt the common fairy dislike of human prying and INFRINGEMENTS OF FAIRY PRIVACY.'

At times the prose gets a little heavy. Here is a little something about the Tuatha De Danaan, which looks interesting enough if you can get past the title: 'The TUATHA DE DANAAN, who were conquered and driven underground by the Milesians and who afterwards dwindled down into the DAOINE SIDHE, were the very cream of the heroic fairies, and their horses were very eloquently described by Lady Wilde in her Ancient Legends of Ireland. (Vol.1. pp.178 and 182–3.)'

However, Cottingley Fairies followers would be mistaken in looking for either recognition or support from this quarter. Mrs Briggs belonged firmly to the 'Doyle was going soft' school, even though the great man produced some of his best Sherlock Holmes stories some three years after the incident. Once more we run up against the old anomaly: when Doyle was writing about Baker Street and those connected with it, he was superb; when writing about fairies or spiritualism, he changed gear, into some kind of feeble-minded dotard, or so critics claimed.

Mrs Briggs ventilated her opinion on radio and in the press, and Frances rang her up to tell her she was wrong.

Frances found the 'plummy Victorian voice' not to her liking, and the two agreed to differ, with the folklorist going back to her forthcoming dictionary, which included such titbits (if one may be allowed to use the word) as: 'F232.2 Fairies have breasts long enough to throw over their shoulders.'

Such reference works are always a useful historical source but a case may be made for the inclusion of ongoing sightings perhaps. I corresponded with Mrs Briggs before her death a few years ago and found her lucid, helpful and tolerant. She was noncommittal on the fairy photographs and felt that any practical fieldwork would invite ridicule or criticism.

In 1972 Stewart Sanderson of the English Department at Leeds University had been elected President of the Folklore Society for a third year and cast around for some suitable topic for his presidential address. The year before, as detailed earlier, Lynn Lewis and *Nationwide* had persuaded Elsie to appear in her living-room before the cameras and tell her story. Sanderson had noted (and later taped) her hesitations and prevarications and considered that the bright 70-year-old interviewee had given enough clues for deductions of fake photographs to be made. He also wrote off to Price's for a copy of their wartime advertisement, which was thought suspiciously to resemble the fairies in the first photograph. Sanderson also contacted Leslie Gardner, who, like his father, had an interest in the case and dwelt near the River Thames. Much of the correspondence between his father, Doyle and the Wright family was packed away in an old blue suitcase; some of the letters were beginning to become over-damp and had partly disintegrated.

The enterprising Mr Sanderson (and he will be blessed by future scholars for his enterprise) persuaded Leslie Gardner – then in his eighties – to donate the correspondence to the Brotherton Collection at Leeds University, where the folklorist lectured. Leslie Gardner also passed over five glass plates which he imagined to be originals of the photographs. It is possible that some are, although a scrutiny of the original two prints suggests that they did not emanate from the negatives at Leeds.

'As I saw him walking away down the path with the letters,' Leslie Gardner once confided to Elsie, 'I wondered whether I was doing the right thing.' I feel that future generations will endorse his wisdom here.

On 21 March 1973 the President of the Folklore Society delivered his annual address, reappraising the evidence in the Case of the Cottingley Fairies. He suggested, with special reference to the tape-recording of Elsie on the 1971 *Nationwide* telecast, that the photographs were not what they seemed. In essence, he doubted very much whether there had been fairies and the girls had snapped them.

He began cautiously, quoting from Piggott's *Flight from Reason* and stressing the need for scientific standards in such a matter. Then he went on to praise gently the prose of Doyle and Gardner in the affair and passed on to an account of how the first famous photograph came to be taken. Here, after some 1,800 words or about fifteen minutes, he fired his first shot. I quote from his address: 'As the black shapes appeared on the plate in the developing dish, Elsie called out to Frances, who was in the scullery, "We've got them; you'll see."' Sanderson then goes on to point out the *double entendre* which might be put upon the phrase 'we've got them' – it can also mean that others have been hooked by a strategy or story, or to 'effectively trick somebody', as he puts it.

Here we meet with an inconsistency. The actual words spoken by Elsie in Doyle's book are, 'Oh Frances, Frances, the fairies are on the plate!' There is no mention of the 1971 *Nationwide* words. And on YTV in 1976 Elsie's words were: 'Then I said to Frances . . . the fairies are coming up on the plate . . . she was dancing outside, weren't you?' At the risk of splitting hairs, as do too many would-be scholars, it seems that Elsie was not employing, to her 10-year-old cousin, such subtleties of innuendo as are suggested.

The speaker continued his address by talking about class distinction and the way in which the Wright family were possibly overawed by the bow-tied, middle-class E.L.G. This is undoubtedly a valid point – Elsie was always wary of hurting Gardner's feelings in any way, and much admired him. 'He was about the only person who ever believed me,' she told me once. Sanderson elaborated upon the occupation of Arthur as a mechanic by trade but made no mention of his ability as a chess-player or a singer, nor that he was always referred to as 'Mr Wright' in the village, enjoying a certain status from being connected with the millionaire Briggs.

To deal piecemeal with other points:

(a) 'It appears that Elsie Wright was employed in a photographers' studio, where she acquired at least suffcient skill to do simple re-touching.'

Elsie worked for six months in the basement of a photographers' in Manningham Lane, Bradford, in 1916, where she ran errands and also 'spotted' photographs; that is, she cleaned away odd spots which appeared on prints. After the hullabaloo of 1920, the photographer was interviewed and had very great difficulty remembering who Elsie was, which reflected the obscurity of her position. She was, of course, unable to process the plates of the two photographs in 1917, and her father developed these.

(b) 'Elsie as a school girl showed considerable talent in drawing and painting: a contemporary, when interviewed, specifically mentioned paintings of fairies.'

The illustrations of Elsie's fairy paintings in this book evidence the strength of this general point made by Sanderson. However, many may have been copied from the illustrations of Dulac and others.

(c) 'I've told you they're photographs of figments of our imagination and that's what I'm sticking to.'

Sanderson regarded these words with some suspicion, but Elsie was using a phrase she employed to Chambers of the *Daily Express* in 1965 and hoped that this would mean that interest in the affair would wane. (However, she had read about the photographing of thought forms, as in some Japanese experiments, and also the significant results obtained by photographing the thoughts of Ted Serios in America, and this began to colour her explanations in the 1970s.)

Sanderson also thought Elsie's manner generally evasive and concluded his reappraisal of the available evidence by giving it as his opinion that the photographs were not what they purported to be.

The last round in the contest of different opinions on the Cottingley Fairies was a personal matter, for some correspondence passed between Mr Sanderson (then Director of Dialect and Folk Life Studies in the School of English at Leeds University) and myself. He wrote politely and not without humour, and hospitably invited me to lunch with him in the Senior Common Room one day.

Stewart Sanderson (friendly fifties and specs) seemed an astute man whose immense scholarship has fitted him well to be president of the Folklore Society for three years in a row. His paper on the Cottingley Fairies was soundly documented and based carefully on written and recorded sources. He argued closely, and his conclusion seemed warranted from the evidence he examined. However, he appeared to limit his sources of data. He used the 1971 *Nationwide* telecast and was not prepared to consider other statements made time and again to the media that there were fairies at Cottingley; neither did he value personal contacts with Elsie or Frances. Furthermore, he seemed to rely overmuch on the testimony of Elsie, without seeking the opinions of Frances. I also mentioned the points of view of fairy-believers.

Mr S. was most polite, for I tend to gush when roused, and this I did. I stressed, particularly, what I called the qualitative element, and the statements by Margaret McMillan and de Vere Stacpoole that honesty shone from the girls' faces. My adversary informed me that it was rather subjective and that he was interested in evidence and logic.

In vain did I move on to the sociology of knowledge and how we are even socialized into habits of logic and thinking and that in many cultures fairies have been seen and widely accepted.

'But not photographed,' smiled my host, and I supped up my wine and thought that it was in the Ivory Tower that knowledge was certainly carefully preserved; and also excluded at times maybe.

*   *   *

In early 1977 I was visited by a reporter from the *Daily Mail*, who told me he had been to see Stewart Sanderson, of the Folklore Society, who felt that the pictures must be fakes. So we appeared in the *Mail* under the headline 'A FAIRY RING OF CONFIDENCE – we never lied in sixty years, say sisters'. The friendly reporter had written of the cousin link but a hasty sub-ed had fumbled.

'Two folklore experts are still locked in the dispute over whether the fairy photos are genuine . . .' ran one sentence. It was pleasant to be thus academically elevated. (Folklore fan – yes; expert – no.)

It's always interesting to reflect on the reality of the interview as opposed to the written report. In this case, it was in the reporter's bedroom at the Dragonara Hotel, Leeds. I had passed the telephone numbers of Elsie and Frances to him, and he was about to ring them up. He just couldn't believe the photographs I'd brought for him to see. Approximate conversation was thus:

'You don't *really* believe these . . . look, they've got 1920 hairstyles. Prof. Sanderson pointed that out.'

'He's wrong. These are truthful women. They've been improved a bit down the years, those photos.'

He shook his head and sucked his fag. 'What would you do if I rang up and they said "Ah, we've been kidding all these years" . . .'

'They won't.'

'Ah – but if I ring them up and this is the biggest scoop I've ever had . . . I learn the truth at last . . . as they get to be older they think they ought to tell somebody . . .'

'They'll stick to their story. The truth.'

He rang up Elsie and Frances and they did just that. (But was it the truth?) I thought it was very obliging of them to allow their evening to be interrupted by yet another newsman.

'How about some money for us all?' I asked, but he stood me dinner and that was that, as he passed away into the night as another puzzled unbeliever. Still, it was nice to be a folklore expert, locked in dispute or otherwise.

It is regrettable that the Folklore Society, and such knowledgeable scholars as Stewart Sanderson, did not take more interest in the Cottingley affair. They, more than anybody else, have a historical if not a philosophical context in which to set such fairy sightings – for others have seen fairies at Cottingley, as well as Elsie and Frances.

A lady from Saltaire told me of four of her friends who were passing by a bridge over Cottingley beck recently. It was nearing midnight, and the clouds shifted, revealing a full moon against the night sky. 'They saw four little figures, all dressed in green, dancing on the rail of the bridge ... they sheltered behind the stonework so's not to startle them but they all saw these four figures dancing and then off they went ... nobody believes them, of course, but I do ...' (It is at points like this that critics rudely enquire as to where observers had come from, what they had been drinking and even whether they could walk – indeed, the stonework would have been useful in keeping them propped up, the more unkind might add.)

So fairylike atmospheres of places must be in the being of the beholder and depend very much on sensitivity.

In my brief correspondence with her, Mrs Briggs wrote that it was very necessary to keep an open mind in the matter reviewed by Sanderson in his presidential address, although she gave it as her opinion that it was perhaps unwise to delve too deeply into fairy expeditions and to concentrate more upon recorded folklore.

In opposition to this view is a comment by Geoffrey Hodson who, after his visit to Cottingley in 1921, rose to comparative fame as the author of several occult books with a Theosophical flavour, notably, *Fairies at Work and Play*. In this, he gives us a glimpse of the 'irresponsible gaiety of the kingdom of fairy' which he describes thus: 'I experienced some measure of the joyful, care-free radiant happiness which seems to be the permanent condition of all the dwellers in the fairy world.' So it was a matter of the Folklore Society continuing to frown upon the whole affair, at least in the early stages of the end of the story. Whether such attitudes will ever be modified will depend, of course, upon the cumulative observations of those who perceive fairy life down the years; with a greater sympathy towards such research and a proliferation of records, it is possible that further country excursions will be encouraged.

One such exercise, carried out in the late summer of 1976, consisted of those largely critical of the fairy-story. It was conducted by the *Calendar* team of Yorkshire Television, and it was the first occasion on which I came face to face with the two heroines of our story.

❧ 12 ❧

A Day Out with
Yorkshire Telly

Television vanishes into the night.
David Dimbleby in conversation with the author

The idea of putting together a twenty-minute updating on YTV of the Cottingley Fairies came up in July 1976 at the end of a phone-in programme I had been doing for Pennine Radio in the studio-cum-cellar of an old wool-merchant's building in Bradford. I had been dispensing astrology to callers, and Austin Mitchell had been a decisive and humorous link man, if sharply critical of my starry comments at times.

As he rattled into place the last advertising cassette, the red light went out and he stretched and yawned. It had been a reasonable hour, and much good cheer had been generated.

'Got any bright ideas for *Calendar*?' he asked me. For

seven years, six days a week, his cheery face had brought news and local events to viewers on that evening news programme. (Now he is an MP and catering for a wider audience, with such books as *The Case for Labour* and *Westminster Man*.)

I thought a bit. For years I had pondered over Gardner's book. I had always wondered ... especially after seeing in 1971 a gentle lady on *Nationwide*, Elsie, seeming to be in two minds about the whole affair. But, somehow, I had an idea that there had been fairies, somewhere, somehow ...

'How about the Cottingley Fairies?' I suggested.

'Cottingley *what*?'

I told him the story. He expressed interest and called round on me the next day. With a newshawk's (and history professor's) eye, he riffed through the books by Doyle and Gardner, took in the contents in a few minutes, and gave his verdict.

'Cut-outs. Fakes. Painted on maybe. Conan Doyle was an old man.'

'You reckon?'

'Yeah. They still living?'

'I think so.'

Thus the tentacles of YTV reached out in August and arranged for a day's filming with the ladies. It was the first time since the twenties that they had been back to Cottingley together, and I was invited along (on Friday 10 September) both as a chaperone for the ladies and to offer my comments.

So it was that on the morning chosen in the late summer of that drought year, I knocked on the door of the house opposite 31 Main Street where the Wright family had lived all those years before. An old friend, Rose, had agreed with YTV that we should all meet at her home, and she welcomed me with a smile.

'Frances is here,' she told me. 'Elsie hasn't arrived yet.'

In I went, pleased and excited that at last I would meet the cover-girl of Gardner's book, snapped looking at a leaping fairy. I shook hands with a bespectacled woman of middle class and height, wearing fashionable denim clothes but with a dash of red and black about the scarf and blouse. Aware eyes, a fine complexion.

I realized that she was not overkeen on the hearty social fudge I was building up, what will all my nodding and smiling and gushing on about How Very Pleased I Am To Meet You and I've Always Been Very Interested ... I withdrew into a strategic silence, sitting down on the settee beside one of the young PAs with whom I'd lunched recently. She was smiling sweetly and intently at successive speakers, conferring concentrated approval on all but nevertheless having a quick glance now and then at her watch.

There was much talk of hotel accommodation, for Frances had been staying nearby overnight. I noticed that the heroine of the fairy-story had a faint Midland accent and spoke forthrightly and with flashes of humour. A formidable character, thought I: for indeed, only recently had she been matron at Epsom College, and she had an air of authority around her.

I disclosed my long-term interest in Matters Occult and found myself blundering into the rigmarole of the need for Objective Research; sounding unreal, pompous and stilted. But Rose and her husband George smile politely, for it is not every day they are called upon to house tellyfodder.

An atmosphere of resigned waiting built up in the

room. Outside, technicians were sitting in cars and brakes, smoking, reading the papers, for patience is a cultivated virtue in their work and they are accustomed to delays.

The producer of the proposed fifteen-minute spot is a bright younger lady, and we talk of the professionalism of Austin and whether it will be possible to find the original spots where ... er ... and conversation swirls on to the long drought and how we may really be going to get some rain at last.

Then Elsie arrives and I jerk to my feet. I am expecting somebody, shall we say, on the mature side, for she must be in her mid seventies, of course. But she looks a good ten years younger; she is wearing fashionable slacks and mod gear and, of all things, a black Gatsby billycock hat on her blonded grey curls. The overall effect is of subtlety, beauty and gentleness. The Scots accent comes as a surprise, the legacy of thirty years or so in India with her Edinburgh husband Frank and other Scots.

The reunited cousins, who had not seen each other for a year or two, chat amiably, with no hint of tension at all. Frances bemoans the way in which Cottingley has become built up, and presently we are oh-so-gently moved outside, where smiling Austin Mitchell, healthy and happy as ever, is conversing with the local ladies. Main Street seems to have a lot of people here and there, and there is talk of the light, whether they should start at the back of the house opposite or go to the beck, and there is waiting, waiting, waiting again.

I form a casual trio with Elsie and Frances. During the day we are to become a permanent threesome, with me acting as a kind of chivalrous chaperone, even carrying Elsie over walls at times.

Off starts the epic, with much walking up and down,

and then Austin is nodding at the remarks and hand-gestures of the producer, who points back down Main Street, so that presently we have our genial presenter walking slowly up towards Elsie's old house and saying to the crouching telly operators: 'It was here, almost sixty years ago, that Elsie Wright and her cousin Frances ...' and on he walks, talking cheerfully and confidently, with the two in question beside me, regarding him benevolently. The shot isn't quite right and has to be repeated, with just the same man doing just the same walk and saying in a vigorous voice, '... almost sixty years ago, that Elsie Wright and her cousin Frances ... they used to play in the beck ... a stream down there, just behind their house ... and it was there that they not only claim they ... *saw* fairies but also photographed them ... in July 1917 ...'

Presently there is a little house-to-house quizzing of those who knew the girls all those years ago. One house-wife wants to get her headband just right for the cameras, and there are sudden great gusts of laughter from the group around Austin, hardheaded Yorkshireman for the day getting down to brass tacks.

'No ... no ... I don't believe it ... we none of us believe it, it were a bit of fun ...'

'Why don't you believe them?'

She pauses, leaning against a doorpost with the sausage mike held near and the cameraman squinting into his lens.

'Well – I've been up all the nooks and crannies around here in my time ...'

More laughter, Austin grins, totally convinced that it was a spoof, to put it politely, which got blown up out of all proportion. Girls frightened to admit it ... bowled

over by important men like Gardner coming from London
. . . now they can't go back on it and, anyway, nobody will
ever be able to say for sure . . .

'Yes – as I say – I know these parts and I haven't ever
seen any fairies, so I don't think there is any . . .'

'And those pictures then?'

'Oh, it was a joke . . . nobody in Cottingley believes
them real.'

I stroll around the village with Elsie and Frances. We
look at gaps where buildings used to be, and Frances
shivers a little. She doesn't like it any more. We talk about
housing development in polite tones, and I excuse myself,
wanting to go across and eavesdrop gently upon the young
PAs who, from their animation, seem to be talking about
something important.

'I think Frances is more convincing than Elsie . . .'

I hear one say and then: 'Only Austin can ask those
questions,' and I marvel again at the delicacy of women in
negotiating social encounters: rarely for them the eyeball-
to-eyeball confrontation.

I join in the conversation. Genial Joe, everybody out
for the day, let's all be friends, look – I'm a nice fellow
and please, please, tell me what you think.

'I believe that they believe what they say,' observes one
dark-haired PA gravely.

'I think Frances thinks she's telling the truth,' comments
the producer.

'You mean that down the years the story has congealed
so that they believe it as truth?'

They agree. I ask them why they think Elsie and Frances
spend time coming all the way up to Cottingley. To stand
up for Truth, I suggest, and they smile a little, humouring
The Nutter.

'Day out. They lead ... ordinary lives ... it makes a change for them ... going on television ...'

More conversations and looks at the sky and watches, and it is decided that we might all go on safari round the corner and across the fields and down to the beck, where they ...

We move into cars, and I find myself in one with Elsie and Frances in the back and me alongside a young poker-faced hire-car driver in the front. It turns out (unusually as I think later) that he is a paratrooper on leave from Northern Ireland and making a few bob extra.

Frances leans forward, showing immediate interest. She was married to a soldier, her father was a Regular of course, and she has a soft spot for all matters military, expressing the opinion that a soldier's job is simply to fight and that poets, in particular, don't go with soldiering. I am tempted to point out the merit of Graves and Sassoon, who threw their medals into the sea at Blackpool when on hospital convalescence there in the Kaiser's War, but decide not to.

I think about the tape-recorder, which I now cradle in my lap. Time is golden, perhaps.

'Mind if I turn this on?' I ask. 'I'm very interested in collecting data.' ... I sound pompous.

They say, jointly, calmly and lightly, that they don't mind at all. They chat amiably and naturally together as the tape circles – about family ties and how the place has changed. When they laugh, which is often, there is a high, spontaneous tinkling about it all, and my fancy thinks there *is* something when the pair of them get together.

'Once I was talking to this doctor's wife,' reminisces Elsie. 'She said "Come on, Elsie, tell us how you did it –

I mean, well, it must have been trickery because ... well
... *you* don't believe in fairies, do you, Elsie?"'

High peals of laughter again. Doubters might say that
the jokers display their harlequin costumes for the benefit
of the tape-recorder, but to me they are amused that the
woman should imagine that Elsie is an unbeliever.

We are interrupted by a neat knocking on the window,
and Elsie winds it down. A youngish, eager housewife is
there, notepad in hand, an appealing look in her eye.

'Are you ... ?' she enquires with delicate feminine tact,
and the warm nod of Elsie, black billycock bobbing,
reassures her. She gushes forth humanly: 'D'you know,
I couldn't sleep all night because I knew you were coming
today ... er ... was it up the old road you saw ...'

'No, by the beck,' confirms Elsie.

'Well, d'you know, when we first came to Cottingley
we bought a plot of land up there because ... it was so
calm and peaceful ... I thought they'd show ...'

Some age-old female wisdom working here, thought
I, but you could say I thought such thoughts just to
make me feel better ... the man is, ever, the measure of
all things.

'Oh, could I have your autographs, d'you think ...'
and the pad is passed back and writing-instruments are
produced. 'Er ... could you put your real names ... before
you were married ...'

Elsie executes a gentle scrawl and Frances scribes a
definite signature; both names slope to the right, faintly
unusual for women.

Our fan hesitates. 'Could you put ...' she searches for
words, and I boldly suggest, 'who saw fairies', which is
firmly appended.

They confess not to be particularly interested or impressed

by astrology, scientific or otherwise, but they obligingly give me their birthdates.

'19 July 1901, about eleven in the morning,' responds Elsie, and again I notice . . . that composure, I suppose you could call it. An air of mystery and gentleness and holding back something.

Frances is as outspoken as Elsie. '4 September 1907,' she responds brightly, with remarks about being an old woman, which accompanying hilarity belies.

Cancer and Virgo. I looked at them with an added interest. Frances has a sort of Virgo face . . . severe . . . and Elsie has a certain jawline I associate with the sign. All of which must seem high nonsense to those not into illuminating books like *Sun-Sign Revelations* by Maria Elise Crummere, and others. For as I was utterly biased in favour of the ladies, so do I intuit that in some mysterious way there are the twelve zodiac signs; they, like us, go ages back, and Man has yet to use them to understand himself and others; and to find that by considering them more human relationships may be eased, for signs of fire, earth, air and water orientate in subtly different ways to people and circumstances.

Watery, mystical Cancer and delicate Virgo, a child of Earth indeed. And one fine day they came together in 1917, I pondered.

The tellyfolk are gathering and conversing, and presently the two young personal assistants come smilingly to us, and the car windows are wound down. Apparently it has been decided to have an interview before lunch and to visit the beck and its slopes in the afternoon. And if Elsie and Frances wouldn't mind just getting out and coming along, please . . .

We all eventually finish up at the back of the house

where the girls had lived in that summer of 1917. Here's a bit of conversation from the tape which will give you a whiff of the proceedings.

Austin: Who actually developed the negatives?

Elsie: My father.

Austin: And you were with him.

Elsie: Yes.

Austin: (to Frances) And where were you?

Frances: I was waiting outside ... dancing ... on the tip of my toes ... breathless ...

Austin: Why?

Frances: Wondering whether anything would come up ... we'd never taken a photograph before ... we were never allowed with a camera, were we?

Elsie: No. That's right. Then I said, Frances ... the fairies are coming up on the plate ... she was dancing outside, weren't you.

Frances: Yes.

Both laugh at the memory.

Austin: Er, did you believe you'd got a fairy on the photograph?

Frances: We hoped.

Elsie: Yes, we hoped ...

Frances: We did believe it because we'd taken a photo-graph ... what you take comes out on film, if it's done right ...

Austin: How did your father react?

Elsie: Everybody laughed ... they all thought we'd played a big joke on them ...

A bit they cut out of tape for broadcasting was Elsie's father's reaction: 'There's some sandwich papers,' he commented. 'You ought to have cleared them up before you took the photographs.'

An examination of the two photos illustrates how the impression may have been formed: on the original sepia print – even allowing for fading down the years, although the nature and amount of fading are problematical – the fairy figures do indeed resemble bits of paper; the awkward point for the critics is that, as photographer Snelling commented on seeing them, there is apparently movement here and there. But, they may respond, how could he tell? The simple answer that the beck breeze stirred three paper figures was not, alas, available until sixty years later.

Buffoonlike, I take Austin on one side.

'Hey – I have news for you.'

'What?'

He eyes me brown-eyed, deadpan. A few phone-ins together have built up a certain humour, and he expects a quip and I deadpan back.

'There was a Third Man ... this young bloke who worked at the photographers' with Elsie. He planned it all. They were in love. Then he went to France and got killed and they've kept it dark ever since.'

He nibbles at the idea. 'How d'you know all this?'

'I don't. That's how Conan Doyle would have finished it had it been one of the Sherlock Holmes stories – the Case of the Cottingley Fairies. All nicely tied up. But in real life it is different. They're telling the truth.'

So was the title of this book born – but a more considered tale from John H. Watson is to be found in the Epilogue.

Six days a week on the box for seven years has sharpened Austin's summarizing powers.

'Put-up job. Cut-outs.'

'You calling them liars?'

Pleasant Austin hesitates. 'People believe what they want to believe,' and back he goes to interviewing.

I hover at a distance, watching the cameramen and the one with earphones and a huge sausage mike, and consider the gravity and concentration of the group. Mr and Mrs Smith, owners of the house, stand benignly by the greenhouse, for Mr Smith grows many blooms, and his garden abounds in plants and shrubs. And sometimes, he has told me, on a quiet afternoon he might be working and he has this sure feeling that somebody has passed by behind him and he turns and there is nobody there; which observation, of course, appeals to me enormously, for there is that about the long garden going down to the beck in terms of atmosphere, say I; others, of course, would take a quick sniff around and declare the opposite.

Presently we all go off to lunch, and a very fine meal it is.

I find myself at the end of the table among genial technicians, whose general opinion is the same as Austin's: a sort of unconscious trickery, ossified down the years into gentle old ladies thinking they're telling the truth. They are puzzled by (but politely non-committal about) my notion that it is all a Big First in Human Affairs. I talk of Galileo, Columbus, Newton and all the rest, who got razzed when claiming to be First-Timers.

'But you can't compare these two old dears with that lot,' objected one.

'They don't look like pioneers.'

'Pioneers never do,' I rejoin, but it is pleasanter to get stuck into the grilled kidneys and wine and let talk drift as to when the banks in Leeds close on a Friday, for there is demand for funds to freshen up the weekend activities.

After lunch we all go off on safari, and the gentle rain begins to come down.

Elsie is not quite sure where we have to stop the car, and the ones behind halt here and there, with, I imagine, adverse comment inside. Finally we confront a black wall with barbed wire over it, and Elsie points to the tops of trees showing in the middle of the field. That is a surprising feature about Cottingley beck: it is a sharp declivity, perhaps only fifty yards across, with fields on either side; it also drops down fifty feet or so, with assorted trees and bushes going down to the gurgling brook.

'I think it's about there that we saw the gnomes, but I might be wrong,' she speculates.

So the strange procession weaves along, with the cameramen heavily handicapped. Elsie and I go over a bridge and stay on higher ground, as the brave Frances leads the main group, with some determination, down towards the waterfall.

Elsie and I are alone by a towering old oak.

'Round about here the gnomes used to come out,' she says, in much the same manner as ordinary folk would talk about the weather. 'I think they've cut down some of them.'

Conversation swings to the sight and sound of such wee folk.

'What did they wear? Did they say anything?

'Oh . . .' Elsie is a bit puffed. 'Russet colours . . . they were a bit shy.'

I shouted to the main party that we'd found one of the spots where a photo had been taken, and the gang half-inched a sliding diagonal way back up to us.

Here is a little more from the tape recorded at the time:

Elsie: When it became clear Frances pressed the trigger on the box camera ... the gnome began to look very clear ...

Austin: Do gnomes come and go?

Elsie: Yes.

Austin: I mean, why didn't you sort of make a grab for it, or ...

Elsie: You couldn't ... it's like grabbing for ... for a ghost or something ...

Austin: What ... what did the gnome do then, when you'd finished?

Elsie: It just used to come ... then ... it just used to come because they were curious ... and then fade off again.

Austin: If ... if you could see them, you and Frances when you were both together ... you're both together now ...

Elsie: Yes.

Austin: Must presumably still be here, if they were here in the first place, why can't can't you see them now?

Elsie: I think it's really because we were only children – we were very young then ...

So the afternoon moves along, with Austin eventually coming to the Big Question:

Austin: Did you in any way fabricate those photographs?

Frances: Of course not.

The ladies (a shade wearier but still merry) went homewards south, and I suppose the general verdict among the crew and production team was that somehow there had been trickery, and nobody would ever know; Elsie and

Frances, it was charitably chatted around, had terminally arrived at a state of chronic self-delusion.

On the Monday I had to go back to Cottingley, and we took various background shots of Austin with or without the beck or walking up the street here and there. He sat on a rock with the waterfall near and said: 'So it was that the figures were simply cardboard cut outs, as you can see here.'

'Where?' I asked afterwards. 'I don't see any.'

'The technicians'll make them.'

Then Austin gravely interviewed me. I chose a middle path: 'I believe that there is an elemental form of fairy life which has been seen by some human beings. When you approach any hypothesis, you must weigh up the evidence . . .'

Elsie and Frances were quite pleased with the programme when it was shown. Their account of their adventures in 1917 and 1920 remained as cryptic as ever, with the point clearly established that they could not confess without seriously damaging the reputations of Doyle and Gardner.

But why not own up – or at least sign affadavits one way or the other? By the end of 1976 Elsie was seventy-five and Frances sixty-nine, and surely, after almost sixty years, the time had come for truth? The answer, I think now, was that both saw publication possibilities and were unwilling to work with each other. Meanwhile, I served to keep the pot boiling and had media and academic connections and had not, as others, attempted to exploit them in any way.

During the day I had told them that I was intent on

solving the mystery, but always within the context of adding to paranormal knowledge, with my occult interests going back many years. At that time my statistical studies on astrology, working with Professor Alan Smithers of Bradford University, were beginning to attract interest. I had addressed the British Psychological Association on our findings a couple of years before. However, my attitude of deliberation was not to the liking of Elsie. Some two years later, in August 1978, when I had come to know her well enough for plainer Yorkshire speaking (if not a frank disclosure as to fairy photographs), she wrote a letter to me (10.8.78) which is still intriguing within the context of the mysterious last photograph:

> ... Joe, not until you leave that solid piece of ground behind that large moss covered rock with its rather solid looking fairies as you stand solidly beside Austin Mitchell mentally mulling over with him his argument over cardboard, wire and paper cutouts as you unfold your fairy wings and take a flying leap in among those see-through fairies in 'The Fairy Bower' photo and start talking from that angle will you convince me that you really believe in fairies. Joe, you are like everyone else, they all mentally run away from those last three transparent figures ... that day up at Cottingley Beck you could have slain Austin Mitchell in 5 seconds from the right angle.

I wrote back assuring her that I was certain that fairies had been seen on many occasions and that, in company with Yeats and others, I believed them to be all about us – as are television, heat, light and delta and gamma rays.

'I came out from my rock years ago,' I responded, 'having publicly championed several causes such as astrology and survival at death ... and fairies.'

I asked her to expand on these remarks, but she did not choose to do so; neither did she ever again appear in the company of Frances on television. As on our day out with YTV, it was Frances who dominated and who was to continue to dominate further debates.

So was the programme neatly presented, with Frances stealing Austin's thunder and coming off the screen as a determined individual who claimed to have seen fairies and claimed that the photograph had not been faked. In retrospect, of course, it is easy to think of questions that *might* have been asked, such as, 'Is this a photograph of actual fairies dancing? Did you hear any music? Are these cut-out figures?' But, as ever, hindsight brings sharper perspectives.

The YTV technicians zealously constructed cut-outs – the opening shot was a grinning Austin looking at the camera over the top of these, and he told watching viewers how the sprites were 'cardboard figures on metal frames', whereupon minds all over the West Riding began to ponder on how Elsie might have acquired wire, tools, time, expertise and the privacy for such a deception.

The following week I was at lunch with friends and we were discussing the pros and cons of fakery, with me suggesting that the onus was now on critics to say how the photos had been faked and by whom. Opinion was veering round (as it did with Kodak) to Elsie's having had some sort of help, and the waiter joined in our debate.

'I saw that programme . . . I thought those photos were fakes until I saw Austin Mitchell twirling those cut-outs round on that bar . . . there has to be a backing for figures when you're photographing them . . .'

And on the debate swirled, and I heard again the merry laughter of older ladies from the back seat of the car hired for the day ... was it mirth at human bickering ... or was it something more? I determined, more than ever, to keep in touch with Elsie and Frances, to keep visiting when I could, to keep writing ... If they were deceivers, I reasoned, why tolerate me? And why tell me there had been fairies?

So was I determined, more than ever before, to continue investigating. As was another researcher on the other side of the Atlantic.

✖ 13 ✖

The Amazing Randi Attacks

Mr Randi and the Committee for the Scientific Investigation of Claims of the Paranormal have put the photos through some image enhancement, a computer process used to increase the definition of pictures . . .
New Scientist, 10 August 1978

Randi is a skilled entertainer and a brave man. In 1979 he endured entombment in a block of ice for an uncomfortably long period, although some may suggest that the igloo may preserve bodily warmth – but no matter, there have been other daring feats accomplished by this unusually fit individual.

He was initially riled by Uri Geller. Detecting, instinctively, that part of Geller which was showman and illusionist, he showed how some of the feats could be replicated; alas, the psychokinetic side of Geller's performances, which are proven beyond all doubt, he ignored.

A parallel might be drawn in the case of the Cottingley

Fairies. The photographs mostly have an 'improved' look about them, which, of course, does not mean that fairies were not there. Bearing in mind the many subsequent observations of fairies from independent sources, it is possible that they were. However, Randi cast around for somebody who could have done the improving and, as in the case of other critics, deduced from the prevarications of Elsie mentioned by Stewart Sanderson in his address to the Folklore Society that this might have been done in the Wright household.

Means of enhancing photographs to pick up greater details – it amounts to moving the picture very slightly and rapidly and rephotographing, I am told – had been developed in connection with moon pictures in the seventies, and Randi, aided by other interested parties, notably from the *New Scientist*, subjected Gardner's reprints to enhancement. What was found was made clear in Randi's book denouncing various 'psychic' impostures, but snippets from findings were published in the *New Scientist* dated 10 August 1978. Matters were reported thus:

> Mr Randi and the Committee for the Scientific Investigation of Claims of the Paranormal have put the photos through some image enhancement, a computer process used to increase the definition of pictures of the moon, for example. Image enhancement can show up details that are captured on the photographic image but which, because they are blurred, are not visible to the eye.
>
> CSICP member Robert Sheaffer and colleague William Spaulding applied the technique to the fairy photos, lo-and-behold they found among other evidence of fakery, the strings holding up the fairies.

All of which sounds pretty damning stuff. A sample of

a headline from a local paper gives the jubilant tones of critics: 'Just a fairy story, says the computer' (*Bradford Telegraph & Argus*).

It fell to me by chance, to acquaint Elsie with the content of the *New Scientist's* column. Bearing in mind that this was billed by them as 'the Great Exposure', her manner was matter-of-fact – rather as if I'd said, 'Oh, there's an interesting bit in the paper here about roses . . .'

She was amused on the whole. I pointed out that the rather poor reproduction (most unscientific for a scientific publication) showed streaks between the fairy offering harebells to Elsie and the sky, with the word 'STRING?' (as opposed to 'STRING!') scrawled thereon by some rigorous member of the CSICP. Elsie said she wondered in what particular part of the sky such invisible string could be hung and, anyway, assuming that they could find invisible string from somewhere, wouldn't the ever-present slight breeze in the beck cause a model or figure made of paper/cardboard (wire-framed, presumably) to sway?

Randi, however, or one of his associates, had learned how Fred Gettings had happened upon *Princess Mary's Gift Book*, published in 1914, and fastened with relish upon p.104, for there, for all to clearly see, was a picture illustrating a fairy poem by Noyes – which bore a suspicious resemblance to the much-publicized Photo One. (The poem on p.104 the CSICP chose to ignore – supporters, of course, would say that this was far more important than the picture and represented, symbolically, the reverse of what critics were trying to show).

He wrote to Elsie, saying that he had rumbled her game, and suggested that she privately confess all and he would make it as easy as possible for her. This is a variant of 'Leave the country – all is found out' which, it is imagined, would produce a reaction in many of us if such was received. Randi also wrote darkly that Elsie had obligations to confess once and for all and that it was in her interests to do so ... Elsie replied briefly, telling him to do his worst, and put his letter on the fire.

One Stephen Biscoe, of the *Yorkshire Post*, thought he was on to a scoop and, after writing the piece 'Computer Kills Off Fairies', he hurried down to see Elsie one Sunday morning. To his chagrin, she prevaricated gently, as was her wont with enquirers, and told him he'd have to make up his own mind. She politely offered him lunch, but he declined and returned north, a baffled young man.

It is, perhaps, too simple to talk about those for and against in the case of the Cottingley Fairies. Elsie, particularly, rather disliked all the intermidable arguments backwards and forwards and always said that people had to make up their minds for themselves.

So James Randi, middle-aged American stage magician and escapologist, was only making up his mind on the evidence available to him when he declared the pictures fakes and, therefore, the girls tricksters. Above all, perhaps, he is irritated by those who are taken in by what seems, to him, a simple trick.

This attitude is echoed in Charles Higham's book on Doyle, published in 1976. The case is summed up thus: 'Actually, upon close examination, the appearance of the photographs, which are palpably fake, suggests that rather shaky copies of the Price night-light fairies were pasted on to the negatives. Whatever the technique, the fabrication was done after extraordinary skill; exactly who was responsible for it is still not clear. As recently as the 1970s the Wright sisters were interviewed on BBC television, and persisted in claiming, in their old age, the complete authenticity of the photographs.'

This Price's night-light theory is something of an old chestnut. The *London Star* wrote that Price's said the figures in the first photo were 'an exact reproduction'. Doyle, on the other hand, said he wrote to Price's, who said they weren't.

The Price tableau bears only the slightest resemblance to the first print; but Higham makes reference to 'the photographs', thus extending his analysis to the other prints, which have no links whatever with the advertisement.

In 1980, Randi published his conclusions on the Cottingley affair, suggesting that Elsie had added wings to cut-out figures, some of which had been copied or partly copied from pictures elsewhere. Any notions that fairy life had been observed seemed an absurd impossibility to Randi, and also to Asimov, a notable science fiction writer who wrote an introduction to Randi's book, *Flim Flam: The truth about Unicorns, Parapsychology and other delusions*. (Lippincott and Crowell, New York, 1980). Hence there was no discussion as to the constant assertion of Frances that she saw fairies.

Yet Randi, following Gettings, made a valid point as to Elsie's ability to copy (or embellish) figures or rural scenes. Her illustration in the plates section of fairy life by a stream clearly owes, let us say, a debt to Dulac in terms of setting, foliage and some figures. Hence critics can contribute useful perspectives, as sociologists may draw attention to the social construction of events and interactions between people involved.

It is to the dramatization of these by a young playwright commissioned to write a BBC television play that we may next turn.

❧ 14 ❧

Dramatic Interludes

The pen is mightier than the crowbar.

Elsie Hill

If any one great truth is to emerge from the curious case of the Cottingley Fairies, for me it is this: that human beings are fallible, vain and consequently in social life prone to gloss over their imperfections and present themselves as favourably as possible to others. Such uncomfortable ideas are echoed by the current sociological concepts of bounded rationality and opportunism: we don't know as much as we think we do, and we tend to delude ourselves and others in the causes of credibility and status. So are our potentials to worship at the fairy shrines of Truth and Beauty curtailed by a harsh world.

By the summer of 1978, promises for the denting of future reputations were calmly building up. I had been headlined in the *Daily Mail* as championing the ladies and their photographs, opposed by the folklore expert Stewart

Sanderson. ('We never lied in sixty years, say sisters,' ran the headline.) Randi and the scientists firmly backed the computers and moon cameras and the deductions that strings in the air had held up the fairies. Brian Coe of Kodak had written to me saying that the fairy photos had seemed to him so like those of Arthur Wright 'stylistically' that he would have said they were 'by the same hand'. And, through it all, Elsie and Frances continued to maintain that they had seen and photographed fairies.

Both were especially pleased that year, for there were indications of a Hollywood interest in their story and a play commissioned by the BBC had come to fruition.

At the back of their minds (or perhaps the front) I now realize with hindsight that both ladies were much concerned with the money (perhaps huge sums) to be made when their revelations might be published on a world scale, notably in terms of screen adaptation.

'I've heard it said that every hour, somewhere in the world, somebody makes a reference to the Cottingley fairies,' Frances once told me. Elsie, also, thought in terms of a worldwide secret being spectacularly disclosed, though on her own terms of course, Frances merely benefitting financially.

Yet down the years the episode had solidly resisted any form of dramatic adaptation. Leslie Gardner, following on from his father's example for half a century, had discouraged any further follow up studies, and the correspondence down the years was mostly in the possession of the Gardner family. As has been mentioned, it was not until the prestigious Stewart Sanderson of the Folklore Society arrived in the scene that an ageing Leslie decided to release the crucial letters; notably from Polly Wright and Edie Wright, confidante of Elsie in 1919 and the go-between linking the Bradford Theosophical Society and the parent body in London as represented by Edward Gardner.

In what dramatic form might the tale be cast? Elsie, like me, had musical comedy leanings and more than once we thought in stage terms. The very setting ... sunlight on a stream and fairies dancing ... the charm of girlhood ... the scorn of adults ... all these constituted a potent background, exhaustively used on telecasts. (Even the worldly Austin Mitchell had appeared from an introductory miscellany of woodwind strains, misty circulating figures and sunlight through the branches.)

Then there would be the matter of the plot and, inevitably, the dénouement. In 1978 this was four years distant and critics of fairies maintained that the unmasking of deceivers should be a main theme: champions favoured a more open minded approach, but what of dramatic interest? And we who favoured some musical treatment pondered without success on possible songs to futher plot twistings ...

In the middle of the year I read of the arrival of Virginia Chase in a local paper. She had a Hollywood background and had written a film script of the Cottingley saga which she showed to Elsie and Frances. I had some conversations with her (she, too, was a believer), and she saw her film as potentially successful worldwide. Since that time I have not heard from, or of, her, and I suspect that her proposed piece, culled in parts from the books by Arthur Conan Doyle and Edward Gardner, was without either commercial appeal or even plausibility – Houdini jumping into Doyle's sports car and the pair of them zooming off to London was only one of the inaccuracies of circumstance, for example, that I noted. But Virginia was good-hearted and hard-working, much liked by Frances, and we may hear more of her.

More professional than Virginia, perhaps, was the young Barnsley playwright Geoffrey Case, who contacted me in 1977, saying that the BBC had commissioned him to write a play on the Cottingley affair. I quote from my letter to him dated 14 April of that year – Elsie had agreed to the play being written but Frances had reservations: '. . . Frances is prone to second thoughts in all directions. Mind you, she is also a straight talker of Yorkshire blood, and objects to phoneys. I have a great respect and affection for her and I suppose that if she sticks out to the bitter end it will be hard for you. But the situation is not without hope: Frances may have second thoughts, on the assurance of anonymity, and her appreciation that you are writing on a *theme* rather than at the usual Did They Or Not level may help.'

Elsie in particular enjoyed all the socializing, and an extract from her letter below reflects the eagerness we all have for dramatic interludes, notably where the media are involved. She wrote this to Leslie Gardner 18 April 1977:

> Young Mr Case spent a very pleasant afternoon with us, you would like him, the idea is a children's play based on the Cottingley Fairy Story. Frances I think liked him too, he asked if I could phone her and ask if it was all right if he could visit and talk to her.
>
> I did this, giving a glowing account and that he was a one time actor and now a playwright and a most handsome and good looking young man.

So we sorted out differences, and Case wrote his play, which was filmed at Cottingley and elsewhere in the summer of 1978 and produced by Anne Head.

The ever-present element of farce latent in our case surfaced briskly as filming began in the back yard of 31 Main Street and elsewhere. Errant juveniles would toss objects from a distance to disturb matters, and there were the usual sloping hazards as cameramen, actors and actresses (both young and old) scaled banks and foliage in search of televisually aesthetic backgrounds and scenes. With relief, I suspect, did they return to London studios for indoor shots.

Frances took an increasing interest in the production, passing on to Anne Head her own manuscript of her journey from South Africa, her arrival at Cottingley and her descriptions of fairy life there. Together they watched the first showing of *Fairies* as BBC2 Play of the Week on Wednesday 20 October 1978.

Randi and his fellow members of the CSICP (Committee for the Scientific Investigation of Claims of the Paranormal) were outraged that no prominent statement emphasizing that the photographs had been proved to be fakes followed or preceded the play.

Anne Head did not follow up the claims of Frances in any way, preferring to let the fairies fade away, as it were. There was some subsequent follow-up in a Richard Baker morning chat show, where Frances and the older Katharine Briggs became involved in dispute, and there the curtain on Geoffrey Case's play went down. Like me, he believed that fairies had been seen and photographed by Elsie and Frances, influenced perhaps by various articles I showed him. In particular, Walter Clapham had written at length in *Woman* after interviewing the ladies, and boldly entitled his article 'There *were* fairies at the bottom of the garden'.

Similarly, we discussed the article by Shaw Desmond

from *Prediction* 1937 headed 'Fairies do exist', in which the Cottingley data might be subsumed within the context other fairy sightings. (See also Chapter 6 in my book *Modern Psychic Experiences*, Robert Hale 1989.)

After the visits of Virginia Chase and Geoffrey Case, Elsie herself felt the urge to compose a play. Here, without introduction, is what she wrote:

The Case of the Cottingley Fairies

'OPENING SCENE'

ACT ONE

The mischievous fairy Puck slips through the opening in the stage curtain and stealthily tip toes to the edge of the stage, he then flicks his thumb back, and says, 'There's a mixed bunch of people back there, mostly newspaper reporters, and they are all trying to prise open a great big oyster shell, but it's unopenable after sixty years, it's crusted up through old age.

'But they all know that inside there is a most interesting pearl.'

The pearl contains one of two things.

(Either a pearl bursting joke)

(A lustrous pearl of beauty) capable of whisking people's imaginations off to gorgeous and precious fairy land places.

Puck laughs merrily and flicks his thumb back once again, saying, 'Just listen to them, can you hear them heaving and grunting as they are all trying to prise it open, some of them have got crowbars, and two of them are having to go with a hammer and chisel.'

Then the strong light that has been illuminating Puck, fades out, and we see him no more, and the curtains swing open, and we see the thick crusted old oyster shell, it's about six feet wide, most of the men have shed their coats and as they sweat and struggle, only one man is standing aside with a pencil poised over a note book. Someone jibes at him for not helping, he says, 'I want to be the first to get it down on paper when the mystery comes unstuck.'

One hot and sweating worker yells, 'Hey!, did you hear that chaps? This guy has been just standing there with a pencil in his hand while we have all been slogging our guts out,' to which the young writer replied:

'The pen is mightier than the crowbar,' where-on the whole crowd of them down tools, put on their coats and disperse, one loud last remark from one of them saying, you can blooming well prise it open with your pencil then. The writer now all alone with the giant shell, climbs up and sits down on top of it, then replaces his pen and writing pad to his pocket and then with elbows on his knees he sits in sad contemplation.

Then to his astonishment, two wings expand from each side of the shell and away he floats.

Curtain falls on (ACT ONE)

For me, this short scene is an important clue to the true and inner feelings of Elsie. Elsie was a dreamy and romantic child and a sensitive and compassionate adult. In her last interview with the media, two years before her death and on the occasion of the death of Frances, she was asked to comment on her belief in fairies and firmly denied their existence. I would question that this was her true opinion. I believe that the odd, Barrie-like ending to this short scene suggests that Elsie was well aware of a form of fairy life almost within human perception.

Tantalizingly unavailable are the conversations between Elsie and Frances in that summer of 1917. All that I have is the remark of Frances to me when we were writing together. '. . . What would you say if I told you that Elsie had never seen a fairy?' and the words of Rosie who had been a close friend of Elsie.

> When Frances came they seemed to shut themselves off totally. They wouldn't let anyone go with them up the beck.

Could it have been that the eager and sensitive younger Frances was trying to create conditions under which Elsie, also, might see fairies? And there were remarks of Elsie to Gardner that it was necessary to sit still and 'entice' the fairies. Had there been no fairies to see, and Frances had used them merely as an excuse for rural exploration beyond the normal bounds, I do not think Elsie's short play would have been couched in these terms. The eventual translation of the writer (thought to be a composite of myself, Case and Libe) is certainly nearer to the lustrous pearl of beauty (the levitation of the scribe into the realms of faery and beauty) than a 'pearl bursting joke' revealing that Elsie ridiculed those who believed in fairies.

In short, the play fragment suggests to me an outlook nearer to the mystical than the material – to some overarching benevolent force of Nature, rather than the harsh world of the atheist. Elsie's later dismissal of fairies was, I guess, the device of a tired and ailing old lady not wanting to be bothered by reporters any more.

But such, needless to say, is my own subjective view – my own construction of social and metaphysical reality, if you have a stomach for current sociological verbiage. It is interesting that such phenomenological approaches are creeping into the current fieldwork of business studies no less than the more familiar social science fields of enquiry. In the quickening field of fairy research in the early 1980s such interpretive studies began, unwittingly perhaps, to proliferate.

One such subjective report came from a forester: Ronnie Bennett, formerly a wrestler, who had seen fairies in the vicinity. (Given his earlier vocation, it was pleasing to see how open-minded folk were in discussion with him on such a controversial subject.) We sat in his Land Rover with the tape-recorder going, looking down from the high point on Round Hill where he had parked; down on to the golf course below, the Aire winding west to nearby Bingley, and over on the other side of the canal the hills rising up to over Ilkley way. West Yorkshire viewed at its best. Here are some of the things he had to say; with a little of me:

R.B.: When you've worked with yourself a lot of years, you see things Nature-wise. If you were to go down into the local and tell people what you've seen, they'd laugh at you every day ... I've been head forester here, now, going on twenty years ... two of us have been sitting here having our drink of tea when a fox came down and, by Jove, if my mate hadn't moved his arm I think it'd have taken a sandwich out of his box ... that's giving you one example, and I'm also showing you the atmosphere that we're working in.

Self: Very interesting.

R.B.: I can also ... start to tell you things ... a very respectable citizen, around this area, walked through these woods and one evening after he'd walked round he said, 'Well, I wouldn't like this to go any further but I wouldn't dare repeat to

149

anybody outside what I've seen in Cottingley Woods . . .

Self: What d'you think it was that he *had* seen?

R.B.: I thought he saw the fairies. Because I have men who work for me and they're the same . . . I say to them, 'All right, you can snigger and laugh – that's up to you . . . you've only been here five minutes. I've slept here all night long, many times, I've been here at two, three, four in the morning . . . the figures and shapes you see is nobody's business . . . most of it is in the imagination . . . but only humans can do you any harm . . .

Self: Yes. I think humans do far more harm than anything else.

R.B.: That's right.

Self: Have you ever seen any ghosts?

R.B.: Er . . . no . . . well, I've *thought* I've seen them . . . I don't know why I should see them . . . I don't believe in an after-life – when you're gone, you're gone . . .

Self: Yeah.

R.B.: As far as Nature's concerned, I think I'm as close to it as many'll ever get . . . to get back to what you've come about . . . I have places in this wood where I've seen Cottingley fairies . . . now, the remarkable thing, and this is what might surprise you . . . people have asked me, old friends of mine, come on what're they like . . . and I said what d'you think they're like and all . . . every one . . . has it in their minds of what these gnomes are like in your garden . . .

Self: Yeah.

R.B.: Now the remarkable thing that struck me what I saw was very similar, and I swear on my life if I never get out of this Land Rover again . . .

Self: Yes . . . (Laughter from both of us.)

R.B.:   What I saw . . . was very similar to the photograph you sent me . . . I was astounded when I opened it and there was this photo of a lady . . . and I don't know those two sisters . . . apart from the little bit of literature that you sent me . . . and that was very small . . . and there's one lady there and there's this fairy . . . I was nowhere near as close as that . . . there weren't many seconds . . . I didn't make conversation . . . and I didn't see one, I saw three . . . and I didn't sleep for three nights after I'd seen what I'd seen . . .

Self: Whereabouts was it in the woods?

R.B.:   Well, we're not far off . . . I brought you up here to give you some idea . . .

So my research boat beat on against many currents.

❧ 15 ❧

Research Directions

The photographs cannot tell us much. It is the people who must be checked up on.

Sir Oliver Lodge

At the mention of research, the thoughts of most people drift towards laboratories, and men in white coats, busying themselves with complex measuring-instruments and, of course, green screens and keyboards endlessly processing information.

A flavour of this popular attitude came across in the Arthur C. Clarke television programme in May 1985. The distinguished scientist from his base in Sri Lanka had decided on the solution of our fairy-story: two village kids . . . a joke that got out of hand . . . Doyle fooled. (The pattern had become something of a cliché.)

ITV, however, sought to inject a scientific slant as to how the mystery had been solved. The phallic tower of Leeds University was shown, and talk of prints in the Brotherton exhaustively examined, followed by the confessions of the ladies in early 1983 and with a little something from the *Princess Mary Gift Book* thrown in – this mixture seemed satisfactorily to dispose of the affair. Geoffrey Crawley, editor of the *British Journal of Photography*, appeared briefly, speaking of Midg cameras and cut-out stiff-papered figures. It all seemed to have been wrapped up nicely.

I watched the programme, hardly expecting any mention, of course. I have appeared fitfully in the media in connection with astrology and matters psychic, but here I would have been an embarrassment, for those of us who believe in fairies would not have been welcome on such a programme.

I was pleased, therefore, to receive a copy of the *BJP* and an article by Crawley a few days later. In the May 1985 issue he had an article entitled 'Cottingley Revisited (at last the low-down on how Tinkerbell was exposed and became a media event)'. In his covering letter he generously wrote: 'The article in the enclosed Journal really brings the matter more or less up to date and you will see that I have been careful to mention your contribution to the clearing up of the mystery.'

In his elegant piece, our benevolent editor had this to say of the activities of myself and Fred Gettings: 'The writer is usually credited with having cracked the case but in fact did little more than pull the threads together on a carefully researched background. It was the artist Fred Gettings who first noticed the similarity between the draped dancers in the Princess Mary's Gift Book and Elsie's Fairies. It was Joe Cooper who provided the first sight of the "prototype print" of the picture and who managed to extract a partial admission . . .'

*　　　*　　　*

Crawley had earlier produced ten articles ('That astonishing affair of the Cottingley Fairies') for his own journal from December 1982 to April 1983. In these he meticulously considered details of the cameras used by Elsie and Frances and their ensuing photography together with the biographies and adventures of all concerned. The disclosures by Gettings and myself thus appeared too late for Crawley to comment in his earlier articles but the fourth boldly headlined us thus:

SENSATIONAL DEVELOPMENT – AN ADMISSION

Students of synchronicity will ponder upon the production of significant Cottingley contributions appearing at the same time: I had no idea the BJP were printing the series until they appeared. Any more than Crawley knew of us.

But Crawley rejected the confession from Frances as to the leaping fairy in Print C being hatpinned to a branch and the fairy offering harebells to Elsie in print D being attached to foliage. 'This Journal believes the evidence is so strong in support of the conclusions that C and D are superimpositions that Frances may now mis-remember.'

Crawley was later proved to be wrong and generously acknowledged this – a measure of his stature as an expert and formidable editor and researcher. Brian Coe, Kodak expert, was in error when he wrote to me saying that Arthur Wright was probably involved. The *New Scientist* and Randi were wrong about the strings. Gardner, Doyle, Snelling, Barlow and myself were wrong about the photographs being of fairies, albeit retouched. Polly Wright and Annie Griffiths were wrong when they believed their daughters to be truthful.

In short, human fallibility was yet again decisively demonstrated, as the need to tolerate all and try to put our emotional prejudices on one side. But this is not easy. Passions have ruled actions in human affairs and these often simmer below surfaces. Victorian Britain seemed staid enough, with its impressive public buildings, the majestic pomp of royalty and the rigidities of the board schools, the clergy and the gentry, but underneath were brewing social volcanoes to blast holes in our twentieth century as trade rivalries bred wars: the millions of war-dead since bear mute testimony to the need for more realistic analysis in terms of power structures and underpinning pervasive emotional ideologies.

Those who purport to analyse social and human behaviours in our times seize on variables which can most easily be quantified. Door-to-door sociology, for example, with a businesslike clipboard and neat questions, seems promising, as does rat psychology, with the luckless experimentees swimming to their deaths at the drop of a stopwatch. But what of consequential advantages from such activities?

It is important, then, to pay closer attention to our subterranean deeps; more than that, all of us yearn for heavenly heights ... rich layers of fantasy, dreams and hopes, causes, the glory of love – these are the prime variables of importance to humans. It has been left to the poets and novelists, on the whole, to shift an appreciation of these beyond the commonplace. The time has come to broaden our concept of the scientist beyond that of the mere physical; the social and psychic varieties are surely increasingly in demand in our volatile times.

And, of course, there are matters of magic, fairies, angels, religion and all manner of psychic variables, which are generally unrecognized by physical scientists, two-thirds of whom are materialists, according to Gallup (1982).

Fred Gettings, amiable middle-aged scholar and far more than the artist Crawley labels him, has no doubt of the importance of mystical intangibles and, indeed, research in relation to such. In a letter to me he wrote: 'I believe that all research, like any human activity, is involved with what we call "magic" . . .'

Over lunch at an Italian restaurant in Keighley some time later, I took up this point with him, but he was on the enigmatic side. A dark-haired European (he spends more time out of Britain than in it), he is one of the most profound of humans. He is, for me, the true scholar in a very old tradition, and his excellent book *A Dictionary of Astrology* (1985) is surely a classic work.

In conversation he told me how he came across the *Gift Book* when working on a history of nineteenth-century book illustration.

'I'd had my mind open for such material for ten years or so,' he told me. 'I had sensed what the girls had been up to, and it was only a matter of waiting for the evidence to turn up.'

He had written his article on the way in which Elsie had copied the Shepperton pictures, but nobody had wanted to buy it in Britain. He had sold the article in America, where it had come to the attention of Randi, who publicized it without any reference to the work of Gettings.

'I've always thought Polly played a much more important part than is supposed,' I said, and he agreed. 'Polly and Elsie were as close together as most mothers and daughters, and it was Polly assuring reporters that her daughter was telling the truth that really tipped the scales, I think.'

'Misplaced clairvoyance' was Gettings' verdict, but on the subject of fairies he was noncommittal. I suspect that he found me on the gushing, simplistic side, but we had an amiable enough lunch, and he agreed with me that the media were more comfortable disregarding the probability of people ever having experienced fairies. Herbert O. Yardley would have found him good company ...

My imperfections as a researcher soon came to light in the late autumn of 1976, after the YTV programme. Elsie and Frances welcomed the idea that I should try to write something on the fairies, and they accepted – at least at a surface level – that I was their champion; but they must have come across many wanting to get to the truth of matters, and their reasons for not chopping my stem have since come to seem faintly curious to me.

Frances said she had written 15,000 words sounding like a medical report, detailing coming to Cottingley and seeing the fairies ... and Elsie was genial and sympathetic and said I should come down to her home for lunch to discuss the matter further.

But when I arrived on Elsie's doorstep, complete with tape-recorder and the zealousness of one who supposed he was championing two much-maligned older ladies, I was small beer indeed. Without effort, she prevaricated gently, and we talked much more of the social texture of Edwardian Bradford and the difficulties of working-class life in the last century. One older relative, for example, could recall being carried, asleep and in the dark of the early morning, on his father's back up the three-mile hill to the coal mine on the heights of Wibsey. Once there, he would pass ten hours underground opening the doors for the pit ponies and their load to pass through.

She would recall her own father, Arthur Wright, telling her what it was like to be a lad in the cotton mills of Bradford in the 1870s and the depression . . . no wonder that the impetus was to learn as many trades as possible, including that of electrical engineer and motor mechanic. And, as I said earlier in this book, economic individualism is to be found in the beings of most of those who live in and around Bradford. Which, of course, breeds a competitive spirit and a liking, a relish, for combat, whether it is getting the better of journalists or freewheeling through lunch with a sociologist and his tape-recorder.

It was always a light relief to get out my ukelele and strum along with Elsie joining in. Frank, her cheery Scots husband who had survived being torpedoed in World War I and later directed the activities of crowds of labourers in India, confessed that he was baffled by the whole affair. It could have been that he was baffled by other aspects also: the credulity of me, the faiths of Doyle and Gardner, or the faint liking his wife seemed to have for publicity, unlike Frances. I failed to find out if he knew the truth of the matter.

In the warmer months we would sit under the tree in her front garden, going through a solid family album. There would be photos of India, Canada, America and a younger Elsie, with near film-star looks, clad in a straight-shouldered uniform when she helped to repatriate ex-prisoners in India from the Japanese camps.

Now and again we might suddenly come across the notorious first photograph, and I recall two comments she made – which may well reflect my gullibility but, because there may be a hint of something else at the back of it all, I give them as she said them to me:

'D'you know, if we hadn't seen the fairies I don't think

I'd believe this photo either' and 'That leaping fairy jumped up five times ... the photo's blurred because Frances is throwing her head back.'

Or I might attempt an earnest interview:

Me (Purposefully): Can you remember the first time you saw fairies?

Elsie: No.

Me: Who saw them first? You or Frances?

Elsie: I think we both saw them together ...

Me: You weren't surprised at all?

Elsie: No. I don't think so. No.

Me: What did they look like?

Elsie: They were sort of ... smudgy through the grass ... you know, you're not quite sure and then they'd gradually take shape ...

Me: Yeah.

Elsie: There's a sort of feeling then it's like that. [Laughs] You had a feeling of them standing and staring and moving away ...

Me: How far away were they? Did they keep at a distance?

Elsie: For a while. Then they gradually got brave ... they were about fifteen feet away for a start ... each time we went up, we'd see them nearer and nearer until they were as in the picture you see with Frances ...

I often used to ask her if she wanted to write about it all, and she would mention again the short story she had put together, called 'The Long Blether' (the last word being a Scots word for verbosity). It was, she said, the moral of the Cottingley Fairies story. 'The fairies were wonderful and I try to forget all about them. You get tired of talking about them down the years. But they seem to be pulling me back – pulling me back towards the ideas I put down in "The Long Blether". That we're all one, and if we don't come together there won't be any of us left.'

On the one hand it could be seen as an older person reacting against the prospect of nuclear extinction. But it could also be seen by the imaginative as the moral at the end of the most prolonged and fanciful fairy-story of our times, I suppose. I reproduce the tale at the end of this book and the first act of a play she wrote on pp.146–7 which emphasizes yet again the fanciful streak in our smiling deceiver.

She had kept the media at bay with ease down the years. She corresponded with Leslie Gardner, son of E.L.G., from 1971 to 1979, writing long letters on many matters except the Cottingley affair. The Theosophist's son was, I believe, more than half hopeful of writing a book about it all, perhaps in harness with Lynn Lewis, who produced the *Nationwide* episode in 1971. In Elsie's account to him of the episode, she stresses that the fairies were 'figments of her imagination', a phrase later to be used exhaustively.

Photographs in the plate section give an idea of how they looked as young girls and later in 1921 when Geoffrey Hodson came along to use his powers of clairvoyance. Elsie was much amused by the one of herself and Frances with Hodson, where she looks at the camera as a rather deadpan 20-year-old, accustomed by then to more than a year of being questioned and questioned.

Our conversation ran approximately thus:

'Look at this one. Fed up with the fairies.'

'How d'you mean?'

'Well, I look fed up, don't I? I was so tired of saying

the same things over and over again, it got to be boring.
Frances looks fed up too.'

And her mind flicks on to a detail of fashion.

'Look, I've got a slave bangle on. It was all the fashion
then, wearing slave bangles.'

'May I borrow this photo and make a copy?'

'Certainly.'

So Elsie was co-operation itself. Her conversation on
tape serves to indicate the gentle and natural flow of her
talk. Her conversation was unguarded and friendly, and
she seemed unconcerned as to whether people believed
her.

But as a researcher I failed – in three years I learned
little more from Elsie about the fairies at the beck.

In contrast to Elsie, Frances did not seek media attention.
I went down to Ramsgate, where she lived in some
splendour in a flat of the Georgian building she owned,
and I encountered a sharp mind and waspish humour. She
was a widow, ridden with arthritis but quite active in social
and civic affairs. She bemoaned the lack of intellectual
or amusing company but was sustained by visits from
and to her children and grandchildren, whose coloured
photographs adorned her walls.

Her relationship with Elsie seemed curiously distant to
me. She frowned upon the latter's delight in chuckling to
newspaper men but supported the stories of real fairies
actually photographed. I remember one conversation I
had with her which went something like this:

'Now then, Frances. Let's imagine it's the vital Saturday.
Elsie has the camera, and you and she walk down the
garden path. What happened at the beck?'

'Well . . . it was like waiting for a bus. We waited . . .

until they came along ... and then we photographed them ...'

I would press her for more details of the other photographs, but always she would come back to the phrase, 'It was a long time ago ... a long time ago ... I don't clearly remember ...'

And doubts might come to me, and I would try, in best scientific fashion, to balance yeas and nays. Frances spoke of the masses of notes she had on fairies but showed no inclination to show me these.

'I think it would have all died down if Elsie hadn't wanted that gnome photograph,' she once said. 'Elsie thought that, as I had a photo with fairies, she should have one as well.'

She was the most hospitable of hostesses. She would also regale me with tales of her days at Cottingley, notably the boredom on Sundays, the black bread of wartime, and the shadow of warfare that hung over the place, for 1917 had been Passchendaele year, of course. Then came the emergence of the *Unexplained* and an invitation to write three articles updating the Cottingley affair. These appeared in the early 1980 issues, and I attempted to present a balanced view, even though I inclined towards a belief in fairies at Cottingley photographed. Elsie and Frances both expresed themselves satisfied with my write-up, and I sent them £40 each for the information they had supplied. In the last article I wanted to show my bias but, fortunately for me, Peter Brookesmith suggested that I take a comparatively neutral position.

I finished my piece thus: 'The critics – Lewis of Nationwide, Austin Mitchell of YTV, Randi, and Stewart Sanderson and Katharine Briggs of the Folklore Society – all these are fair minded individuals interested in balancing probablity

on the available evidence. This extremely delicate balance
did seem to have shifted in favour of the ladies' honesty
during the 1970s but, obviously, many points could still
be elucidated by further research.'

It was at this time that I was commissioned to write a
book on telepathy by the publishers Constable.

Such, in retrospect, I see to be the can-opener which
resulted in the spilling of the beans.

❧ 16 ❧

Confessions

There are things you should know.
A telephone message from Frances, August 1981

A marked feature of Frances and Elsie in the ten years I knew them was their tendency to have only minimal contact with each other. There would no doubt be phone calls as to how much of the true story had been admitted to various magazines, but meetings were only occasional, perhaps because of their living at a distance from each other. Frances was especially keen on getting the market rate for articles, as evidenced by her forcing up the price of one for one woman's magazine; when the *Nationwide* telecast was made in 1971, she inferred from a shot of a home for older Theosophists that Gardner's takings from the widely selling 1946 book had been used to finance this. ('My father did not make a penny out of it all,' Leslie Gardner once wrote to me. Possibly true, but he gained much in terms of status in the Theosophical Society, as did the latter in terms of the proceeds from his book.)

So it was that by 1980, with Elsie seventy-nine and Frances seventy-three, the Cottingley story was still a mystery, in spite of Randi and the invisible strings of the *New Scientist*. The play by Geoffrey Case on BBC had served to keep the pot boiling, but the ladies still stuck to their story: that they had seen fairies at Cottingley and had photographed them.

By the summer of 1981 I was making vague attempts to get a book together, but it was all uphill. I was fascinated by the bulky collection of letters in the Brotherton Library and looked upon myself as a champion for the two of them. I had been for tea with Dame Jean (Lady Bromet), Doyle's daughter, who had risen to be an Air Commodore of the WRAF. In her impressive Cadogan Square flat, with a massive portrait of the great man looking soberly down on us, she told me how she would sit under his desk in the twenties while he wrote. In an earlier letter to me she had written: 'As far as my own opinions of the Cottingley photos are concerned I've a completely open mind. I was interested in your reaction to Frances. It's like UFOs – unless you've personal experience or know someone well who has, one's opinion isn't worth much.'

For, in spite of all debates, I was convinced that Frances had seen fairies. There had been her reference when we first met to '15,000 words like a medical report' about them, and I reasoned that, had it been a joke, she wouldn't have bothered writing, let alone keeping it for sixty years. Furthermore, her daughter Kit totally believed her and was, in fact, researching first-hand accounts of fairies in Ireland, rather after the earlier efforts of Lady Gregory and Yeats. Their book, *Visions and Beliefs*, which details half a hundred experiences, is generally totally ignored.

But at that memorable time I was also working on a book for Constable, who had commissioned me to produce some objective volume on telepathy – not an easy task. I was approaching it from a scientific view: sound data, prudent argument and critical analysis – the ancient sequence which goes for everyday science as we wait at a bus stop attempting to predict and control; or at a physical science level, where variables, dependent, independent and intervening, are known. At a social and psychic science level, of course, the sequence is more cryptic and tortuous. Another obstacle to study is The Establishment (the Church, universities and media), which does not yet recognize social and psychic science.

I had often talked to Frances of my difficulties, and she had sympathized generally with my views. She would again and again come back to Gardner in 1920: 'It was all too rushed . . . they wanted to get it over quickly . . . if they'd spent more time they would have found out a lot more,' she would say to me. Yet she did not offer to pass over her precious 15,000 words at any time – only giving me the occasional interview at Ramsgate, when it would be an amusing occasion with plenty of wine and food flowing and rich reminiscences of Cottingley 1917 or the flapper days of Frances in the 1920s, in which period I was born and by which I have always been fascinated.

In late August 1981 I had an interesting phone call from Frances. We talked of my telepathy book and the hard slog of authorship (I can never decide whether it is the most glorious sport in the world or the hardest labour) and hopes of publication in June 1982.

Then Frances said, 'Can you come down to Ramsgate some time? There are things you should know.'

I paused, a small needle moving somewhere. Not for a moment did I think in terms of admissions of fakery. It was the 15,000 words that read stuffily on fairies that I thought of – obviously Frances had been impressesd by Constable, publishers of Shaw, de la Mare and other eminents. I had found them the most agreeable of benefactors. Perhaps my Cottingley book was to be beefed up after all.

I arrived on a Sunday in early September 1981 – late in the evening, after the long journey down from Yorkshire and tapes playing twenties music to which I am addicted. I had high hopes of interesting descriptions of fairy life at the beck.

But Frances wanted to leave it all until the next day.

'I want you to take me to Canterbury,' she said, and so it was that the next day, a sunny one, I parked the car and we walked to the ancient cathedral at her request.

'I'm just going in here for a moment. You wait in that coffee bar on the other side of the road.' I thought it all a bit odd, but went over the way and lined up a frothy coffee for her return.

When she came across, she seated herself opposite me, hands on chin, a thin, amused mouth, and brown eyes behind round specs regarding me intently. I was talking about other fairy accounts and the trees and streams and types of fairy life, I think, but she interrupted my flow.

'What d'you think of that first photograph?'

My mind flicked to the world-famous snap of Frances and the sprites around her as she looked at the camera, and I thought of the first, untouched sepia print, yellowed and with blurred figures and wisps around her head.

'Well, they've certainly changed your features almost beyond recognition. And touched up the fairies – perhaps from the *Gift Book*. I'm interested in what look like ectoplasmic whiffs around your head . . .'

Frances eyed me with amusement. 'From where I was, I could see the hatpins holding up the figures. I've always marvelled that anybody ever took it seriously.' Again the brown gaze held mine.

My world shifted a little and I had no words. Hatpins. Of course. Now no longer.

'That first photograph has always haunted me. My heart used to sink when I would see it. I swore to Elsie I wouldn't tell anybody.' So had the staunch soldier's little daughter kept her word down the years. Perhaps a prayer in the cathedral had freed her from the bond.

Speech came back to me. 'What – why are you telling me?'

'Last month Glenn confronted Elsie with the Shepperton picture and said she'd copied cut-out figures from it.'

'You mean Glenn never knew?'

'No. He persuaded Elsie to confess in the end. Then he rang up Kit, my daughter, and told her.'

I rummaged into my memory. 'Kit – Christine . . . she always believed the photograph to be genuine . . . of real fairies . . . I . . . you . . . told me she collected accounts . . .'

'Yes. She believed. Then she rang me, and I thought that, as Elsie had told Glenn, I could tell you. And you have a link with Constable. We can write a book together.'

I gulped coffee, pondering with accelerated pulse. God. The truth at last. I thought of my three articles in the *Unexplained* and blessed Brookesmith for insisting that I write it up neutrally.

'What about the other four? Are they fakes?'

'Three of them. The last one's genuine. Elsie didn't have anything ready, so we had to take one of them building up in the bushes.'

'So that's the first photo ever of real fairies?'

'Yes.'

'And Elsie copied them from the *Gift Book* illustration?'

'Yes. I'd brought it over from South Africa when I came to Cottingley in 1917.'

Another pause.

'So we're going to write a best-selling book.'

Frances grinned. 'If there's a book in it. We can try.'

'Do you want to involve Elsie?'

'No. The first she'll know will be when a fat cheque drops in her lap.'

In vain did I insist that the viewpoint of Elsie should come into it. But Frances was adamant. No Elsie or no book.

It was fascinating trying to find a title for our book first of all.

'It's got be gripping,' I told Frances. 'More books sell by their titles and covers than you would think. I fancy two girls ... mistylike ... and a few nature spirits ... plenty of greenery ...'

But Frances said the beck had to be at the centre of it all. 'We want a title with water in it. The beck brought the fairies ... and the sunshine. They were never there in the dull and cold weather. I only saw them in the summer.'

And so we would juggle words and phrases around, often collapsing into laughter, for there was always plenty of wine and spirits in the flat. In particular, I admired the gleaming antique brass fender and white goatskin rug before it. I mentioned to Frances that Elsie had once written about a Cottingley type, very houseproud, who shoved the cat away from her white rug because she was breathing on the brass fender and misting it up. Then I went on about brass fenders as status symbols and remarked that in Cottingley 1917 competition for social status was keen.

'And it was our relatives too,' observed Frances. 'The day we arrived in April 1917 – we got there in the morning, coming from Plymouth where we landed from South Africa – Aunt Polly and Elsie welcomed us, and then in the afternoon we went by tram to the other side of Bradford to see Uncle Enoch's house . . . very posh. It was there that I saw the brass fender and white goatskin rug. Just like this one.' I marvelled at house fashions changing so little in sixty years. 'Yes – I always wanted a brass fender and a sheepskin rug.'

Then we would try to get down to planning our book. Frances said she didn't think there was a book in it.

'You could get the whole lot in about six pages really. I mean Elsie and me and the photographs. Your bit about Gardner and Doyle can't take all much up. What else can we put in?'

'Other people who've seen fairies maybe.'

A pause. 'Well, that isn't about the Cottingley Fairies, is it? I suppose we could pad it out with me coming over from South Africa and the games on the boat. Or before that when we lived in Johannesburg. Going out to the opera . . . it was wonderful . . . I had a little fur cape – my father was a sergeant major in the Army and we had servants . . . it was horrible coming to Cottingley and wartime and black bread and sleeping all crammed up with Elsie in the attic . . .'

Then I might play my ukelele for a while, and Frances would sing 'Bye Bye Blackbird' in a somewhat reedy voice and regale me with tales of being young in the twenties and doing the Charleston. She could also shimmy and do the hoochy-coo and in those flapper days had put the fairies well out of her mind.

She was an excellent cook, notably of meat dishes. I would loaf around in the kitchen while she cooked, and she would reminisce about her family days with her husband, Sid; theirs had been a happy marriage, with their two children, Kit and David.

'They used to like coming in the kitchen when I cooked. It was a sort of family meeting-place.'

All in all, then, our progress on The Book was slow. I took some of her notes and tried to write them up in some sort of Frankenstein fashion, sounding like a little girl looking back, but Frances thought it all sounded phoney and wanted it rewritten.

'Perhaps I'd better write it,' she concluded, so again she got out her newly purchased typewritter and tried her luck.

And still we were stumped for a title. *Fairy Water. The Magical Stream.* Frances wanted something about *Sparkling Stream*, but we never made it.

One thing that particularly intrigued me was her interest in soldiers and her dislike of 'long-haired lefty poets' such as Graves and Sassoon. Her father had displayed much discipline in both the Boer War and Flanders – on his leave at the end of 1918 he had brought home photographs of where their big guns had blotted out German positions.

Frances conceived the idea of writing in the third person and put it thus: 'He would meet her from school and tell her how arithmetic (which she didn't like) was essential in

setting the guns so the shells dropped in the right places.'
She told me that on one occasion she was driving behind an
Army vehicle, open at the back with young soldiers gazing
out, and that she deliberately refrained from overtaking it
for miles so that she could enjoy the interchange of jeers
and good cheer. Frances was somehow steeped in Army
life: her husband was a regular WO as was her father when
he retired in 1919, when he had acquired an outstanding
reputation as a somewhat rigid disciplinarian.

Frances couldn't remember much about that particular
Saturday in July 1917 when she and Elsie had gone down
the garden path to take the famous first photograph.

'It's so long ago. I wanted to forget it all. When you
want to forget something, it goes from your mind. I don't
think they were cardboard – stiff paper.' Such ultimately
turned out to be the case. 'How on *earth* anyone could
be so gullible as to believe that they were real was always
a mystery to me.'

She thought that Geoffrey Case had her wrong in the
BBC play about them in 1980. She wrote to me: 'I was
not the quiet little misery he made me. He 'got' Elsie nicely
but I was a treader on feet, breaker of China, jumper of the
four bottom stairs and was always being "shushed".'

The flavour of Frances as I found her was sharp,
tough, mercurial, waspish, impish, blazingly honest and
hardworking. She held right-wing political views and
despised pacifists.

So 1981 shifted to 1982 and the progress on Our Book
was slow indeed. I tried to write it in the first person
like Frances, and that flopped. Frances didn't like being
the odd one out when my agent came into matters and
wanted agreements signing, and found an agent of her

own. Unknown to me, they approached Gollancz, but they, like Constable, couldn't really see an interesting book in it, especially as Elsie was not to be involved.

Frances became discouraged. 'Perhaps there isn't a book in it.'

Our whole joint authorship project seemed to be sagging, and I experienced the feeling of stalemate which has so often prevented progress in research projects. Ideas, initially so appealing, begin to lose their gloss as grim needs for sustained efforts creep in, to say nothing of appraising market appeal. I had journeyed to London to see the publishers of my telepathy book as to their possible interest, and nobody had heard of the Cottingley Fairies. And all the photos were such obvious fakes . . .

The *Unexplained*, I was told, would come to an end early in 1983, and by July 1982 I made up my mind. Both Elsie and Frances wanted to write their own stories and were stubbornly against any co-operation. I felt, pompously perhaps and with self-glory never too far away in some subconscious recess, that my prime duty was towards knowledge and towards those who, like myself until the awesome conversation with Frances in the Canterbury snack bar in September 1981, believed all the photographs to be of genuine fairies. I would write up the truth of the matter as I knew it so far.

I informed Peter Brookesmith of my intention, and he welcomed my decision. He also commissioned an article from Fred Gettings as to how he came across the Shepperton illustration in the *Princess Mary's Gift Book*, and our articles appeared in the December 1982 issues of the *Unexplained*. ('Cottingley – 'At Last The Truth.') Frances and Elsie stonily severed contact with me ('Tha's properly muckied tha' ticket wi' me!') wrote Elsie in simulated broad Yorkshire, while Frances curtailed our last phone conversation as I have earlier described.

It was Frances who decided to be the first to make a public confession following the *Unexplained* articles, and she chose to telephone *The Times* for such an occasion. Subsequent interviewing produced a modest piece (9 April 1983) headed by the well-known retouched first photograph and somewhat ungraciously headlined:

Photographs confounded Conan Doyle
COTTINGLEY FAIRIES A FAKE, WOMAN SAYS

Then followed a straightforward account of how stiff paper cut-outs and hatpins had been used, but Frances maintained that the last photograph was of real fairies, taken by herself.

When we were writing together, I had drawn her attention to Doyle's written comment as to the navel in the gnome photograph being suggestive of births in the elemental kingdom umbilically similar to our own. I pointed out to Frances that such a dot might be the end of a hatpin, and she was most amused by the thought. Obviulsy she had passed on her enjoyment to *The Times* reporter (without acknowledging the source of her information, of course), whereupon in the newspaper confession matters had been marginally escalated:

'Desperate for evidence of the paranormal, when he saw what was actually a hatpin holding down a cutout illustration of a goblin, he described it as evidence of a fairy navel; proof, he told fellow researchers, that the creatures reproduced in the same manner as humans.'

Elsie at first refused to comment on the article but later softened and had a reporter and a cameraman round at her

Nottingham home. There she was snapped in the very act of cutting out a fairy figure from Bristol board paper. As to the last photograph, she commented: 'It was a brilliant idea. Frances was not there at the time and I just saw a way to take it. I have never even told my son and husband how I did it all. I will swear on the Bible that my father had nothing to do with it, but I will not swear on the Bible that there are real fairies.

And a last wistful comment, 'I am sorry someone has stabbed all our fairies with hatpins.'

In a later issue of *The Times* (9 April 1983) Geoffrey Crawley, editor and director of the *British Journal of Photography*, commented thus upon the questionable last photograph: 'The fairy bower is easily explained by certain technical indications, first noted by Coe (of Kodak) that it is an unintended double exposure of fairy cutouts in the grass. That is why both ladies can be quite sincere in believing that they each took it.'

And in the same letter to *The Times* our worthy photographer disclosed the reason why it was that so few subsequent investigations had been carried out in our odd case since the death of Doyle in 1930: 'Access to the Cottingley material was then barred by Edward Gardner and later his son, in whose possession it remained, and it has only become available in the last year or so.'

❧ 17 ❧

Rose Fyleman and
the Cannon's Mouth

There are fairies at the bottom of the garden.
A phrase used by the Royal Corps of Signal
to denote the sighting of the enemy

The notion of a poetess linking fairies and the battle-field must seem bizarre to most. In 1917 the war news was at its worst, yet it was a fairy incident that caused the upset of the year in the Wright household. A little soldier's daughter, uprooted from the warm security of Cape Town, suddenly came to know food shortages, boredom, cold – and fairies. If we are to believe Frances and a score of other fairy-reportings, manifestations seem most commonly to occur to solitary girls as some form of marginal solace to ill-fortune. 'Pack Up Your Troubles' was a musical source of hope for soldiers, but the eventual suicide of the composer may symbolize the grim ways of the world intersplicing our fairies.

The connection came upon me obliquely – as with much else in this curious case. In 1976 I was corresponding with Leslie Gardner. He held dear the memory of his father and had been involved at the edge of the case in 1920. He it was who had taken the marked plates to be developed, and he had met Doyle, who showed him his new motor bike, which he described as 'absolutely spiffing'. Our correspondence always had uneasy undertones, and when I wrote to him in 1977 suggesting that his father might have got one or two dates wrong in the 1945 book, he wrote back saying, 'Please consider our correspondence closed.'

In an earlier letter he had finished with a phrase that set me off on the path covered by this speculative chapter. He asked me if I knew that: '. . . the poem "There are fairies at the bottom of my garden" was inspired by Cottingley'.

A little digging in Leeds Reference Library revealed that he was, in fact, mistaken. The poem first appeared in *Punch* in the issue dated 23 May 1917 and runs as follows:

FAIRIES

There are fairies at the bottom of our garden!
It's not so very, very far away;
You pass the gardener's shed and you just keep
    straight ahead;
I do so hope they've really come to stay.
There's a little wood, with moss in it and beetles,
And a little stream that quietly runs through;
You wouldn't think they'd dare to come merrymaking
    there – Well, they do.

There are fairies at the bottom of our garden!

They often have a dance on summer nights;
The butterflies and bees make a lovely little breeze,
And the rabbits stand about and hold the lights.
Did you know that they could sit upon the moonbeams
And pick a little star to make a fan
And dance away up there in the middle of the air?
Well, they can.

There are fairies at the bottom of our garden!
You cannot think how beautiful they are;
They all stand up and sing when the Fairy Queen
    and King
Come gently floating down upon their car.
The King is very proud and very handsome;
The Queen – now can you guess who that could be
    (She's little girl all day, but at night she steals away)?
Well – it's Me!

Altogether in 1917 Miss Fyleman, who wrote 'Fairies', had nine poems published; I think it worthwhile to give the complete list with dates:

23 May	Fairies
13 June	The best game the fairies play
4 July	There used to be fairies in Germany
11 July	I stood against the window
18 July	Have you watched the fairies?
5 September	The Fountain
3 October	Yesterday in Oxford Street
24 October	Visitors
5 December	White Magic

It is something of a coincidence that these poems should appear at exactly the time when Frances arrived in Cottingley and admired an English spring. An even greater coincidence is that the first seven lines of 'Fairies' actually bring to mind the setting at the back of Elsie's house at Cottingley.

After I discovered my oddities, I spoke to Elsie about it. (Those with suspicious minds will say, 'Aha! An impressionable girl of sixteen reads *Punch* and the striking poem, and begins to hatch a plot . . .')

'Did you ever have *Punch* in your house?' I asked.

Elsie thought a bit. 'I believe we did. Dad used to bring magazines from Mr Briggs, and *Punch* used to be among them.'

I asked her whether she'd read the poem, and she said she hadn't realized it had first been published in *Punch*. She had, of course, read the poem several times but did not know that it had been written by Rose Fyleman. For the suspicious, my hostess on that occasion answered with the casual honesty which accompanied all her responses to my often rather prying questions.

Back to Miss Fyleman. She was of Jewish descent (link with a theme in Elsie's 'Long Blether'), was born in 1877 (the same year as Polly) and was raised and educated in Nottingham (where Elsie lived). She studied music under Haydn Wood, was a notable singer (links with Arthur) and was a lively, vital and interesting person. I read many of her fairy poems and pondered over these, for I hunch that there is great wisdom to be found in all fairy poems and stories. (One eighteenth-century book I have is called *Tales of the Fairies*, and at the end of each story there are verses headed 'The Moral, just to make sure virtuous points are properly made. The close of this book is similarly traditional.)

She it was, then, who first pointed me in the direction of connecting fairies with warfare – probably the poems coming out when they did and the one called 'There used to be fairies in Germany' set me thinking about it. Then I read a book called *War and the Weird* which was written in 1916 by a serving soldier, and I read of such matters as 'Angels', 'The Uncanny under Fire' and 'The White Comrade.'

And in another book about the Kaiser's War, *The Great Push* by Patrick McGill, concerning such places as Loos and Blighty, there is this unusual poem by an anonymous author right at the front to introduce the book:

> *To Margaret*
> If we forget the Fairies
> And tread upon their rings
> God will perchance forget us
> And think of other things
>
> When we forget you, Fairies,
> Who guard our spirits' light;
> God will forget the morrow
> And Day forget the Night.

Why did he choose that one, I wonder?

Perhaps some can begin to see a few connections: fairies and angels look rather similar; we are supposed to have guardian angels, and perhaps we have fairies who fly around from time to time – the idea of guarding 'our spirits' light' is interestingly linked with the traditional role of fairies looking after flowers; and in wartime, especially in the carnage of the Western Front, life was daily endangered on a dismal and vast scale. Hence in some dim and inexplicable way, fairy poems were passed to Rose Fyleman and so to *Punch* (widely read in France). Psychiatrists, perhaps, may move on to explanations of subconscious hallucinations, to say nothing of compensatory mechanisms.

This strange link between fairies and warfare is echoed also in a poem written by the mysterious Walter de la Mare, a rather staid City gent but known now as a cryptic poet of the very first order, and much underrated in conventional literary circles this century, I feel. This was called 'The Fairies Dancing' and was written a dozen years before the Great War (as folk knew it before 1939):

> I heard the fairies in a ring
> Sing as they tripped a lilting round
> Soft as the moon on wavering wing.
> The starlight shook as if with sound,
> As if with echoing, and the stars
> Frankt their bright eyes with trembling beams:
> While red with war the gusty Mars
> Rained upon earth his ruddy beams.

So will we believe what we wish about the two poems. In his profound book *The True Believer* written in 1951, Eric Hoffer details, frighteningly, how we are emotionally attached to our embedded habits of thought and associated emotions. At worst, fanaticism drives some to violence; at best, we must try to give a chance to all ideas, bearing in mind Bacon's aphorism that we should 'Read not to contradict and confute, nor to believe and take for granted, nor to find talk and discourse, but to weigh and consider.' The wise words written over 300 years ago are as trenchant today as they ever were.

Maurice Maeterlinck, poet, playwright, essayist and psychical researcher, wrote an interesting book in 1913 entitled *The Unknown Guest* in which he speculated about unseen presences from without which might influence human affairs. After considering debates between spiritualists and those who favour subconscious minds at work, he has this to say about those who are outside our plane yet appear from time to time: 'It is infinitely more likely that there is a strange medley of heterogeneous forces in the uncertain regions into which we are venturing. The whole of this ambiguous drama, with its incoherent crowds, is probably enacted round about this dim estuary where our normal consciousness flows into our subconscious.' Whereupon many, including Major Hall-Edwards from 1921 who thought that preoccupation with fairies was unhealthy and perhaps mentally unhinging, would say that it's best to wait until the time comes and find out and not mess about in woolly, world-distracting speculations involving fairies, seances on wet afternoons and all the occult ologies upon which present-day practitioners fatly feed.

Not so Rose Fyleman. For her the fairies are here and now:

SMITH SQUARE, WESTMINSTER
In Smith Square, Westminster, the houses stand so prim
With slender railings at their feet and windows straight
and slim;
And all day long they staidly stare with gentle
placid gaze,
And dream of joyous happenings in splendid bygone
days.

In Smith Square, Westminster, you must not make a
noise,
No shrill-voiced vendors harbour there, no shouting
errand boys;

But very busy gentlemen step swiftly out and in
With little leather cases and umbrellas neatly thin.

Yet sometimes when the summer night her starry
    curtain spreads
And all the busy gentlemen are sleeping in their beds,
You hear a gentle humming like the humming of a hive,
And Smith Square, Westminster, begins to come alive.

For all the houses start to sing, honey-sweet and low,
The tender little lovely songs of long and long ago,
And all the fairies round about come hastening up in
    crowds,
Until the quiet air is filled with rainbow-coloured
    clouds.

But that may be too gooey for some – for others the
parsimony of the two below may be more acceptable:

Who is the third who walks always beside you?
When I count, there are only you and I together . . .
                                        T. S. Eliot

O world invisible, we view thee
O world intangible, we touch thee,
O world unknowable, we know thee.
                                    Francis Thompson

Elsie, of course, linked the fairies with the present world
political situation, as her piece 'The Long Blether' at the
end of this book indicates.

'The fairies at the beck were lovely,' she told me once,
'but I feel as if they won't let me rest. They seem to be
pulling me towards pointing out that all the world is really
one – that we have to look after each other.'

184

So, in fact, the Cottingley Fairy tale is rather like all the other tales of the fairies which were written – there is a moral, and a sombre one, for Elsie in her fable pulled no punches: it is instructive that the one who could be written up as a Bewitching Fairy Godmother in the *Bradford Telegraph & Argus* in October 1978 should be very much down to stark reality with her notions of the dangers of nuclear incineration and the horrors of the last war. And she herself, in India, was, of course, an officer in a nursing corps which cared for prisoners of war who had returned from the terrors of Japanese treatment.

This chapter would be incomplete without some passing reference to the most widely circulated story of angelic beings and the First World War – the reports from soldiers of having seen angels at Mons. But where can one obtain reliable data on this? Eye-witnesses are dead or in their dotage, and heads would shake at old voices describing these bigger versions of fairies.

Had I to choose a single source which, to me, intelligently outlines event and theory, I would choose Hereward Carrington's *Psychical Phenomena and the War*. The author became assistant to James Hyslop, President of the American Society for Psychical Research, and his earlier books were connected with unmasking fraudulent mediums.

Carrington gives some fifteen pages (343–58) to the incident, which he summarizes thus:

> The main outlines of this incident are doubtless too well known to need more than the briefest mention. At the very moment when the German hordes seemed about to overwhelm the British Army, phantom warriors (so the story goes) intervened – English bowmen from the field

of Agincourt – and kept the Germans at bay until the main army succeeded in making good its escape. Such was the report, circulated at the time (August 1915). No eyewitness accounts are given of the bowmen, but reports of angelic intervention are copious.

Carrington gives several independent accounts of both French and British seeing and being uplifted by heavenly beings (petite Jeanne d'Arc, St Michael and St George are most commonly mentioned) but the most impressive description comes from one Begbie, an NCO in the Mons retreat when his battalion was awaiting a German onslaught:

The weather was very hot and clear, and between eight and nine o'clock in the evening (28.8.15) ... I could see quite plainly in the mid-air a strange light which seemed to be quite distinctly outlined and was not a reflection of the moon, nor were there other clouds in the neighbourhood. The light became brighter and I could see quite distinctly three shapes – one in the centre having what looked like outspread wings, the other two were not so large, but were quite plainly distinct from the centre one. They appeared to have a long loose hanging garment of golden tint and they were above the German line facing us.

We stood watching them for about three quarters of an hour. All the men with me saw them, and other men came up from other groups who also told us that they had seen the same thing.

So the forces were withdrawn successfully and Paris was saved.

Opposite the Alhambra Theatre in Bradford (birthplace

of both Elsie and Frances), built in 1914 just before the Kaiser's War broke out, are to be seen two statues. One is of a soldier thrusting forward with rifle and bayonet at some imaginery foe. Tellingly, the years and the Yorkshire weather have eroded most of the bayonet, so that he projects his weapon in the general direction of the new police station opposite. On the plaque beneath him are some suitable words to the memory of those who walked in the sun one July morning on the Somme and gave up their lives that others might shop in the new Arndale Centre just up the hill.

A few yards away is another and rather more ornate statue, that of the diminutive Queen Victoria who, as in all her statues, appears an awesome and gigantic figure. Indeed, no woman before or since has presided over so much effective land conquest. Contemplatively, she holds an orb in one hand and a sceptre in the other. But, oddly, perched cheekily on the orb, is a fairy – not unlike the cut-out figure purported to have leapt up at Frances all those years ago.

To me the two statues symbolize human uncertainties and the possibility of some mysterious, presiding order such as the poets sensed: the deadly bayonet is laid aside and invisibilities rule as in the case of Scott Fitgerald's hero slipping away into Maeterlinck's dim estuary between consciousness and sleep:

The most grotesque and fantastic conceits haunted him in his bed at night. A universe of ineffable gaudiness spun itself out in his brain while the clock ticked on the wash stand and the moon soaked with wet light his tangled clothes on the floor. Each night he added to the pattern of his fancies until drowsiness closed down upon some

vivid scene with an oblivious embrace. For a while these
reveries provided an outlet for his imagination; they were
a satisfactory hint of the unreality of reality, a promise
that the rock of the world was founded securely on a
fairy's wing.

The Great Gatsby
F. Scott Fitzgerald.

❧ 18 ❧

Summing Up

The End of Man is Knowledge.

Robert Penn Warren
All the King's Men, 1947

Any last chapter such as this should pull main ideas
together in answer to leading questions which come
to most minds at the sight of the book's title. In our
famous case I would suggest it is now time to consider
the following:

   a) Did Elsie or Frances or both see fairies at Cottingley?
   b) Why should fairies be seen at that time and place?
   c) Is it possible for others to see fairies? How?
   d) Have any other photographs of fairies ever been
      taken?

Here, perhaps, we should be mindful of Yardley and his
fellow poker-players, impressive with their hats and cigars,
weighing up probabilities. It is thus necessary to weigh

pros and cons and to note, particularly, the reactions of Elsie and Frances to various situations and circumstances. Their capacities for bluffing were extraordinary but, as I shall show, I hope, they had reasons for not wishing to play their separate hands, so to speak.

For Elsie, in 1983 at least, there were no fairies. On 15 April, a few days after *The Times* disclosures, a reporter from the *Manchester Daily Express* somewhat cosily reported an interview with her and seemingly put a stopper on the Cottingley bottle once and for all:

'Mind you,' said Elsie, 'Frances is allergic to the word fairies. But she's a little devil, you know.'

And Elsie herself . . . surely . . . well, just once in a while . . . didn't she believe in . . . ?

'Fairies?' she said laughing. 'No. I don't believe in fairies. Never have and never will.'

A smiling photograph of radiant 81-year-old Elsie accompanied the article, under the headline 'The Biggest Fairy Story Of Them All!'

After the death of Frances at the home of her daughter in July 1986, the latter remarked that her mother had maintained until the end that '. . . the fairies were real: she never changed her story.' In the same *Sunday Times* article Elsie was asked to comment on this and replied: 'There were real fairies, you mean? I don't know what to say. To think it all started with me trying to cheer the kid up and get her out of a scrape.'

Elsie died in April 1988, and her son decided against any press publicity. He is affable, inclined to disbelief in fairy matters and pleasantly agnostic, electing to wait and see. He reads Persian poetry in the comfort of his garden summerhouse, with his wife and young children being disposed to forget the whole Cottingley affair which crept into their lives from time to time. Christine, daughter of Frances, is similarly disposed towards no further comment, although she herself is a believer in fairies and associated folklore.

So it would seem that our famous case is concluded. On balance, opinion has it that the last photograph looks faked and, since the other four were, this fifth appears unlikely to have been of real fairies. Frances, an imaginative child in unfamiliar circumstances and intrigued by seeing the green of an English spring for the first time, would seek refuge from a crowded house of tension by the shimmering beck, and might easily imagine movements here and there. All in all, the Cottingley story seems to have passed away with the deaths of the two Bradford-born ladies.

But here, I suggest we look a little more closely at one or two details.

There is firstly the matter of the letter to South Africa, written by Frances in 1918, which came to light. The *Cape Argus* had published a review of *The Coming of the Fairies* by Arthur Conan Doyle in early November 1922, and a Miss Johanna Parvin, a teenager from the Cape Town suburb of Woodstock, brought into the offices of the newspaper a letter she had received from her former playmate Frances Griffiths, who had lived in Woodstock before going to Britain in the spring of 1917. It is worth quoting the letter in full, I think:

31 Main Street
Cottingley
Bingley
Yorkshire.
9th November

Dear Joe [Johanna],
    I hope you are quite well. I wrote a letter before, only I lost it or it got mislaid. Do you play with Elsie and Nora Biddles? I am learning French, Geometry, Cookery and Algebra at school now. Dad came home from France the other week after being there ten months and we all think the war will be over in a few days. We are going to get our flags to hang upstairs in our bedroom. I am sending two photos, both of me, one of me is in a bathing costume in our back yard. Uncle Arthur took that, while the other is me with some fairies up the beck, Elsie took that one. Rosebud is as fat as ever and I have made her some new clothes. How are Teddy and Dolly?

And on the back of the well-known first photograph are the words:

Elsie and I are very friendly with the beck fairies. It is funny I never used to see them in Africa. It must be too hot for them there.

The point might be made here is that Frances at nine, coming to an English village for the first time, was unsurprised to see fairies since she had never seen England or fairies before. Perhaps she associated one with another. When interviewed by *Woman* in 1975, she had this to say about them: 'I can't ever remember being surprised about seeing the fairies. It never seemed important to us. They were part of our everyday life. We didn't go looking for them, as if on a great adventure. We knew they were there and if the light was right and the weather was right it was just a matter of taking pictures of them as you'd take a view . . .'

Here is the unusual puzzling mixture of possible fact or fancy, but Frances often told me that fairies were seen frequently and became accepted as part of the overall scenery of the beck with its meandering stream and high banks which, even in the 1990s, will still defy the activity of building developers who are poised to erect houses on both sides.

We may assess implications here.

Let us assume that there were no fairies and that Frances was misleading the *Woman* reporter totally. We are forced to the following conclusions:

a) She agreed to be interviewed in order to perpetuate the Cottingley fraud for prestige, money or private personal enjoyment.

b) She mentioned not being surprised in order to buttress her fairy-tale. Perhaps she had read somewhere that children claimed to have behaved thus.

c) She had no scruples as to publicly deceiving millions of readers, some of whom had tender hopes that fairies really did exist and that the photographs might, after all, be genuine.

d) She was something of a skilled interviewee and deceiver. Her words have a disarming casualness about her which suggests a devious and polished background reminiscent of a confidence trickster.

e) She did not, at eleven, shrink from writing a letter totally deceiving a close friend as to both the photograph and the existence of fairies.

Against this, we have a picture of Frances as an honest, determined and blazingly efficient person throughout her life. As the matron of a boys' public school, Epsom College, she had an awesome reputation for straight talking and fair dealing. And in an obituary her daughter commented: 'She could not tell a lie if she tried. She always maintained the fairies were real. She never changed her story.'

Again, let us list deductions from the above statement, assuming no fairies and faked photographs:

a) Frances, having lied to her daughter for sixty years as to the photographs, lied also as to seeing fairies until her dying day.

b) Thus her daughter, who had known her intimately and with whom she had been on close terms until her death, had been totally deceived not only by the Cottingley photographs but by fictitious accounts of fairies.

It is at this point that another important factor might be considered. Both Elsie and Frances had silently observed Edward Gardner and Arthur Conan Doyle making money from publications on the Cottingley affair. After the *Nationwide* telecast in 1971, a home for retired Theosophists was shown, and Frances had mistakenly supposed that the sales of Gardner's book on Cottingley had substantially contributed to this. And in correspondence with me she often touched on the financial capacities of Doyle and on his businesslike dealings in the affair. Thus I consider that both, during the later 1970s, were biding their time, keeping up neutral media comments and hoping for an opportunity when they might give their own unique versions of their Cottingley adventures. Hence their mixed and contrasting statements.

Here is a last anecdote which I cannot imagine will meet

with general acceptance or cross many Boggle Thresholds (to use the fashionable SPR phrase).

In the newspaper obituary (*Sunday Times*, dated 13 April 1986) by Norman Lebrecht entitled 'FAIRY LADY DIES WITH HER SECRET'), Frances' daughter mentioned that her mother had often seen fairies, the last one popping up beside her as she stood at the kitchen sink during the Second World War: 'She was horrified and ran out of the room. The publicity as a child had upset her too much.'

Students of probability, ruminating upon those giving accounts of fairies to a *Sunday Times* reporter may well consider that those who wished to further a belief in fairies generally would choose less extraordinary details, whereas champions would say that such an account supports that the occult journalist Lynn Picknett when she once told a class of mine that, 'The stranger the phenomenon reported, the more likely it is to be true.' However, I would personally construe such a remark with caution, interesting though it may be and certainly relevant in some cases, as in the poltergeist tale I heard of, where toys were found strewn around a formerly orderly nursery and a teddy bear was actually seen walking up the stairs to an attic.

Here, of course, my chapter is in danger of collapsing to the sardonic mirth and irritation of critics; I can only say that all science must start with observables, however incredible, biased, subjective or mistaken they may seem to be, for one can never tell which seemingly odd trails will lead to crocks of paranormal gold.

Elsie's letters to Leslie Gardner, following on from the *Nationwide* telecast of 1971, are masterpieces of bland correspondence on both sides. The son of E.L.G., like

Lynn Lewis, the producer of the Cottingley programme, had hopes of collaborating with Elsie or Frances in producing a definitive book but nothing came of it.

Elsie's son Glenn was kind enough to pass this mass of correspondence on to me, and it is intriguing to read Elsie sidestepping fairy comment and, by contrast, commenting at length on her social life in general. Here is her description in a letter to Gardner of the *Nationwide* interview which some may perceive as shedding sidelights on our search for probabilities in a summarizing chapter such as this:

I could feel all the time that Mr Lewis thought my father must have been involved, but my father, I said, had told everyone who saw the picture, that he was sure that Frances and myself had done the whole thing as a joke and that he thought we had either cut them out of picture books, or I had drawn and painted them myself and cut them out and stood them in the grass. I said it wasn't until later Mr Gardner and Conan Doyle found out they could not have been made this way. I said I would swear on the Bible that my father had nothing more to do with the fairies except developing the plates. Then he asked if they could make a film about it on 'Nationwide'. I was reluctant as I had made up my mind long ago that should we settle back here in Britain again, and the newspapers came after me again, that I would tell them that I believed they were 'photographs of figments of our imagination'.

Some years ago after we had settled here a Daily Express man came, he got our address from someone in Yorkshire, and this explanation cut the conversation short like magic, though my cousin Frances was rather upset when she read it and said, 'What did you say that for? You know very well they were real.' I said, 'Well, you didn't live at Cottingley when the heat of the story was on, you have no idea what it was like, they even came after where I worked, I almost got the sack through their asking if they could talk to me so often.'

However, I said I would go through with the programme on TV and back up my cousin Frances saying they were real fairies, but after the TV programme, if more newspaper men come around, I said, I shall go back to my six shooter words (photographs of figments of the imagination).

Such a letter seems fair evidence for real fairies having been seen by Frances. There is a ring of truth to the account, and an explanation emerges for the ambiguous replies which Elsie was wont to give those from the media who confronted her. Her decision to keep the matter quiet after leaving Cottingley mainfested in her not telling her son until he was ten years old, and never mentioning it to friends in India. She did indeed wish to forget the affair. In a 1972 letter she wrote to Gardner: 'Unlike Frances I much more prefer the role of being a solemn-faced Yorkshire comedienne than being thought to be a solemn-faced nut case.'

Accounts of fairies having been encountered are to be found in books by Arthur Conan Doyle (*Dwellers on the Border*, Chapter 8 in the last book of his life, *The Edge of the Unknown*, written in 1930), *The Boy Who Saw True* by Cyril Scott, *Fairies at Work and Play* by Geoffrey Hodson, and *Your Psychic World A to Z: An Everyday Guide* by Ann Petrie, alias Tara Bonewitz. This last-named writer is specific as to how one might emulate Hodson on pp.68–9 of this book in discerning fairies:

She sums up:

If you want to learn to see fairies, then you must use the sixth sense, be very, very patient and learn to be still. If you go crashing through the woodland talking loudly, disturbing the vibrations, nothing will happen; but if you go to the same spot at the same time each day, treading carefully and with sensitivity, and being extremely quiet, then you will be far more lucky. Simply lying in long grass and feeling the energies of plants and trees will help you attune yourself to the environment. It is really the case of the fairy allowing you to see her and trusting you enough to come close ...

Do leave a corner of your garden wild and leave it for the fairies. All too often we forget these things as we control our immediate environment, lay out our gardens with beds and lawns and don't think of the other kingdoms who share the space with us. Perhaps you, too, will catch a glimpse of the gossamer wing or have a conversation with a gnome as I have.

Few researchers share the patience or zeal of the sensitive Tara and sceptics would draw attention to the lack of interest shown in replicating fairy photographs utilizing appropriate weather conditions and willing sensitives.

However, there are several texts giving examples of spirit photography, whereby discarnate influence has brought about faces or light effects on negatives. Currently the Noah's Ark Society and Robin Foy's research group in Norfolk have produced similarly impressive photographs, which are now attracting the attention of the Society of Psychical Research and are claimed to be the result of discarnate direction.

Fairy perceptions are thus a subtle and personal matter, which is why it has been artists and musicians who have produced the most striking impressions of fairy forms and life. The Fairy Appreciation Society has recently been formed by my friend Mitzi Huxley in Devon and she makes this important point relating to those seeking awareness: 'We who have seen fairies will say to see a fairy one must look with the heart as well as the eye.'

Alas, I am a more earthy being. I have never seen fairies. Worse than that, I don't think I am ever likely to. I'm not the type.

Down the years, from time to time, I have joined parties of eager hikers, tramping over the dales of West Yorkshire. I may have progressed a little from saying 'So what?', as others view panoramas with Wordsworthian enthusiasms, but when it comes to sitting and trying to tune in with my sixth sense, I turn off, become bored, yawn, look at my watch, finish my sandwiches, get uncomfortable sitting on the grass and wonder about my various tomorrows (never my yesterdays, I glory to say).

I fail to develop in development circles, I fall asleep in yoga classes or in the dark of the seance room (where I snore too sometimes). I am overconscious of street lamps outside as we sit there, the traffic going by, and stomachs rumbling. In short, I am not the type for elevating my cosmic consciousness.

I come to life, much more, at the mention of theory. The why. Explanations as to why or how things happen, often at an unsuspected or deeper level. Hence my lifelong interest in the occult, or hidden.

Social science and education both intrigue me. I see them as forms of flowering – developing latent talents and contributing towards human happiness and knowledge, if you like. A first truth of social science is that nothing is what it seems on the surface; hence I enjoy its spicy subversiveness as well as its benevolence. For me, any paranormal issue is embedded in social, psychological and philosophical features, and any paraphysical question must attract an interdisciplinary approach. In common language away from the jargon into which social science all too unfortunately languishes, my questions are, 'Who says what?' 'How do they know?' and, crucially, 'What is the use of knowing?'

Perhaps a diagram is a better way of expressing my educational outlook, where both theory and facts play crucial parts.

My research circle is simplicity itself:

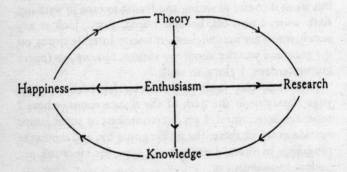

Penn Warren based his character Willie Stark on Huey Long, the charismatic demagogue of the 1930s, and his aphorism which heads this chapter is to me but an intermediary stage in the generation of greater human happiness. For me, the simple finding of the whole Cottingley affair is that the invisibilities of presence attract or repel fairies; in the case of young Frances, her wonder at the English spring and her capacity for aesthetically blending with higher realms after the prescription of Tara Bonewitz brought her happiness and spiritual harmony with nature spirits, as in the case of the score or so I have on tape describing similar experiences.

I cannot resist ending my last chapter with a few theoretical long-shots.

Too often in psychic studies, theorizing has not been bold enough, but then we are accustomed to be, literally, down to earth in our struggles to survive the immediacies of finity. Our infinite fancies – our wild imaginings – these are too often suppressed and many times have I travelled on the swaying subterranean London tube and sympathetically speculated on the dreams of those mutely imprisoned with me. It is no coincidence – but odd, perhaps, that our island race, descended mainly from pirates, should produce major poets, dramatists – and humorists.

Thus the theme of the Cosmic Joker is one which vastly appealed to Peter Brookesmith and Lynn Picknett, editors of the *Unexplained*, which ran for three years and turned out to be one of the sharpest postwar illustrated weeklies on matters paranormal. They commissioned and encouraged my articles on the Cottingley fairies and mercifully edited some of my wilder ideas.

In a reprint of some *Unexplained* articles (*Incredible Phenomena*, 1984), Brookesmith writes thus on possibilities of some higher realm of humour intruding into events from time to time:

> After all, if we play pranks upon one another, why shouldn't the Universe, of which we are but a part, laugh at itself from time to time? And, like a good magician, refuse to tell how the trick is done?

The cosmic joker will, therefore, play most merrily with reality – and with our all-too-human tendency to expect consistency in the world. He will on one occasion appeal to our own sense of humour – causing a truck laden with carrots to collide with another carrying olive oil to make the biggest carrot salad in the world, for instance, or inexorably drawing a man called Phang into a career in dentistry. He will, on the other hand, mock the scepticism of science by dropping an enormous lump of ice out of a blue sky to land at the feet of a distinguished meteorologist, forcing him to accept the inexplicable. No less outrageously, the cosmic joker presents sea monsters and UFOs to photographers, and then causes their cameras to jam for the first and last time.

And on Cottingley:

But the joke may be more subtle than that. What, for example, is one to make of the notorious photographs taken at Cottingley, England, earlier this century? Many critics have remarked how like scissors-and-paste jobs they look. Others may feel that such a trick is typical of the cosmic joker, who would, of course, make absolutely certain that the best evidence for such other dimensional beings *should* seem suspect. That is all part of the prank of tantalising innocent humans with a glimpse of such creatures in the first place. And if humanity insists on taking itself and its ideas so seriously, doesn't it *deserve* to be teased.

My research, if such it can be called, was littered with bizarre and humorous incidents over the seven years or so: there was Frances turning on a bemused Austin Mitchell and asking him how a nine-year-old girl could possibly keep a secret like that for a lifetime; my heaving Elsie over stone walls as tellymen carrying equipment stuggled up and down the banks of the beck in a scene which Heath Robinson would have been pleased to record; Frances driving nails by night into the tyres of the headmaster who had unwisely used her Ramsgate parking space; and the recurring preference of Elsie to be known as a 'solemn-faced comedienne'.

Odd events have come my way in plenty. Besides the fortuitious meetings with Elsie and Frances through Austin, I have known the following:

a) After a lecture in 1982 entitled 'Tinkerbell, are you there?' at Saltaire Spiritualist Church, pussy-willow buds were abstracted from stems and appeared in a neat semi-circle on the polished floor at the front of the hall as we took tea afterwards at the back. Nobody had been near the rostrum, and the operation, if humanly carried out, would have been both curious, lengthy and conspicuous.

b) When I was being interviewed on breakfast television in connection with Tinkerbell 86, an excursion to Cottingley with sensitives (fairy bells were heard), the sound unaccountably went down in London and Guy Michelmore quipped as to fairy intervention. The same day, prior to being interviewed on Radio Two, we had a crossed line and a third rich chuckling voice talking of Pan.

c) After a 1982 lecture at Swanwick I was handed a written report (reproduced below) from a sensitive. (In fairness I must mention that many times sensitives have approached me after lectures claiming that visiting figures have stood beside me as I talked, unperceived by a largely unprivileged audience. These have included Red Indians, Victorian gentlemen, children, Chinese sages and a variety of lights, both stationary and circulating. And, of course, a whole spectrum of colours have been seen, construed variously as tension, humour, sympathy, arrogance, warnings, rigidity, vulnerability and auric oscillations of some kinds.) Here is the report from an earnest and balanced young family man, spending a week in psychic discussions and lectures:

Perceptions by a male sensitive as I was giving a lecture entitled 'Tinkerbell, are you there?' at the Swanwick Conference Centre on 3/4 May 1982.

3rd May
As Joe was talking I was aware of a pale pink energy around his chest then a pale lavender all around him.

Then a female fairy fluttered on to his left shoulder. Also the same colour – a pale pink dress. Pale lavender wings. Cream hair also the same as Joe's. She was holding a stick with three bells on it. Every time he said 'Tinkerbell' she went to the other shoulder. I didn't tell him about this. But I was aware that the energy change attracted this beautiful fairy, also the same colour, from a higher vibration dimension. So I left it to see whether any other thing tied up at a later date.

4th May
Went to Joe's lecture not looking for anything. After twenty minutes I became aware of a pale pink energy around his chest. Then the pale lavender all around him. And the same fairy fluttered around him and went to his left shoulder at this point. I told him. He said 'Is she still there?' I said, 'No. She fluttered off.' She was still there but other people didn't see her. So I felt it would be best to tell him on his own. Every time he said 'Tinkerbell' in the course of his lecture she would change shoulders, holding a tiny stick with three bells on it in his ear.

Note by sensitive
This is not fantasy or imagination. A higher reality tuned into his aura when it was emitting the right frequency and colours. This can only happen when he is in the right state of mind, mentally, emotionally balanced then can pink lavender flow. Pink for love. Lavender for higher levels.

Author's note: To my shame, I do not remember the name of this sensitive in his midthirties. All I recall is that his birthday was in the last decanate of Taurus – around 16 May.

Lastly, (to the relief of many, I hazard) there is the matter of the Pan hypothesis which extended largely to Edwardian England and the second dreadful decade beyond. It is conjectured that the great nature god came near, perhaps sensing hardships to come, that he might strengthen hearts and hopes. The plays of Barrie, the Arcadians of Robert Courtneidge, the curious chapter in Graham's *Wind in the Willows* entitled 'The Piper at the Gates of Dawn' – these are thought to be suggestive of the lesser god's brooding help in raising spirits.

Then there was Chaplin, arguably the most famous man in the world in the Cottingley year of 1917. In his book *The Great Charlie* (Deutsch, 1952) Robert Payne detects strong Pan influences in one of the world's greatest clowns. He positively identifies the famous tramp creation:

It is obviously the great god Pan and even wears, thinly disguised, the goat mask – for what else is the moustache but a sketchy replica of the goat's black muzzle and why the baggy trousers unless it is to hide the cloven hoofs and legs thickly covered with curly hair? We enter a world where the god mimics himself in the pure enjoyment of himself, and there seems neither rhyme nor reason for the doing of it . . . since I am a god or a fallen angel, he seems to be saying, I can do what I damned well please . . .

And on the more sinister theme of the fairy world and extinction, Payne notes that the mask of Charlie suggests not only Pan but also a skull. On taking up this theme with Chaplin, the latter remarked to the author: 'I am always aware that Charlie is playing with death. He plays with it, mocks it, thumbs his nose at it but it is always there . . . there is death in him, and he is bringing life – more life. That is his only excuse, his only purpose. That is why people recognized him everywhere . . . they wanted the ghosts to come and bring them life.'

As we, perhaps, desire fairies to reassure us of pleasanter planes beyond earthly confines; where we may begin to move in the direction of living happily ever after – as in all beloved fairy-tales.

❧ Epilogue ❧

The Case of the Yorkshire Fairies

by
John H. Watson MD

Note to the reader: This is one of the more trifling cases from my records involving my friend Sherlock Holmes, and I append it here as an example of how he could solve such minor mysteries almost without moving from his armchair; in this instance his efforts amounted merely to reaching for a reference book and listening to details for perhaps fifteen minutes.

It was, as I remember, a sultry day in early August 1920 when the odd affair of the fairies photographed in Yorkshire came to our notice.

We had returned, temporarily, to our old diggings

in Baker Street at the request of the tenant who had succeeded us, a young solicitor. In the few years since our leaving he had been disturbed from time to time by callers and past clients and, although Holmes had dealt with many at a distance, there were a few of some urgency which needed further clarification at a personal level. Accordingly, we had come to stay for a month while the young man holidayed, climbing in the Alps, and our first week had been busy.

We were at breakfast on the Monday of the second week when the housekeeper announced that a Mr Edward Gardner was without, together with our dear old friend Arthur Conan Doyle.

Holmes rose swiftly to his feet as the two entered the room. He shook hands with the massive Doyle, who has played no small part in editing my chronicles in the past. The pair conversed pithily upon their interests, Holmes speaking of the difficulties of fertilizing queen bees and Doyle on the uphill task of converting the world to spiritualism, for he was at that time in the midst of a strenuous lecture tour at home and overseas.

His companion, an alert and neatly bearded smaller man of middle age, seemed to be somewhat restless and at last could contain himself no longer.

'Forgive me, but my train for the north leaves from King's Cross within the hour and I wonder, Sir Arthur . . .' He paused, somewhat embarrassed at interrupting the pair of old friends in conversation.

'I've told you before – drop my trimmings', growled the worthy knight.

'Pray sit down, take some coffee and let Watson and me hear all,' urged Holmes.

Once seated, Doyle elaborated upon matters. 'Gardner

here is a Theosophist and president of the Blavatsky Lodge in London. He is also their photography and lantern-slide expert. He has a strange tale to tell and, moreover, it is one in which I may become involved.'

'It is indeed an odd story!' burst out the other. 'It may well go down in the annals of psychic photography as an epoch-making event.'

'Compose yourself, my dear sir,' observed Holmes. 'Today has been a busy one for you. Typing a letter, perhaps in a hurry, a visit to your barber for your beard to be trimmed – no doubt you follow me, Doyle.'

'Letter sticking out of his pocket stamped but unposted. Residue of beard trimmings from the towel on his shirt front and bow tie,' grunted Doyle in his Scots voice. 'But why should he have typed it and in a hurry?'

Holmes smiled. 'When I see an otherwise neat and tidy man with traces of purple carbon on his finger tips, I infer that he washed his hands hurriedly after typing. And only rarely do persons post letters for others.'

Gardner had been looking in growing wonder from one to the other. 'Amazing, Mr Holmes!' he commented. 'You may well be able to use your unusual powers of observation and deduction on these, which I believe to be photographs of genuine fairies.' And so saying he drew a packet from his inner pocket and carefully took out two photographic prints. 'These were sent to me in May of this year.'

Holmes examined them closely in silence.

'They are two of the most remarkable pictures I have ever seen in my life,' continued the Theosophist. 'I beg you to regard them with an open mind. They were taken some three years ago by two children who have seen and played with fairies since babyhood. They are cousins, and live in a remote Yorkshire village called Cottingley.'

We watched with interest as Holmes swept a slender hand to a side table and took up a powerful lens, through which he scrutinized the photographs for some minute or so. Finally he passed them over to me. 'Dancing fairies and a gnome, Watson.'

I stared at them curiously. On one print a girl looked at the camera, with fairy figures on a bank in front of her. A blurred waterfall appeared to be in the background. On the other print a young lady sat on a grassy bank under some trees, reaching out her strangely elongated hand to what seemed to be a gnome.

'I, too, had them under a lens,' commented Doyle. 'I would draw your attention to the umbilicus of the elemental, Holmes. Do you not think it points to birth in the fairy kingdoms having certain physiological parallels with our own?'

Holmes smiled. 'I have no data on such things. Tell me, Gardner, who else inhabits this household besides the cousins?'

'Their mothers, who are sisters. The master of the house, Arthur Wright, is the husband of one, and dwells with his wife Polly and daughter Elsie. In 1917 her sister Annie and daughter Frances were staying in Cottingley while her husband fought in France.'

'It is a long time for such photographs to come to light,' mused Holmes. 'Three years ago, you say?'

'I understand that the father was so astonished by what he saw that he kept them on a shelf in his dark room for eighteen months,' confessed Gardner. 'He is an artisan, and doubts their truth. The mother is, happily, a Theosophist and believes them to be genuine. Both are of the typical honest and straightforward Yorkshire working-class type. I have been to interview them, and my report is with Sir Arthur. Today I am hoping to go north for more photographs of fairies from them.'

'And how are you involved, Doyle?'

'The *Strand* wants an article on fairies for their Christmas number. I hope to use these prints. But I have my doubts, Holmes, I have my doubts. As have Lodge and a few others, who imagine them to resemble Californian dancers.'

Holmes rose to his feet and paced to the window, gazing down at the motor traffic which had increased disturbingly since the late grievous war.

'I take it the sisters wear hats, Mr Gardner?'

The Theosophist looked puzzled and, I fancy, a little dismayed at my friend's seemingly odd question. 'Of course.'

'Secured in place, no doubt, by hatpins. I fancy one such was used to impale our gnome to the ground and your umbilicus, Doyle, may be the point showing through. And the bank, or mossy rock, is not only at a convenient height for the younger girl to rest her elbow but is also just the place to set fairy figures, similarly secured.'

'Great Heavens!' burst out Doyle. 'What a fool I have been! And, of course, the gnome lacks a hand – the clumsy use of scissors, perhaps!'

'Or the extremity became detached when carried in a pinafore pocket,' suggested Holmes. 'Mark you, Doyle, these figures are finely executed, and my guess is that unusually sharp scissors may have been on hand. Was one of the sisters a tailoress, Gardner?'

The bearded Theosophist's jaw dropped. 'Annie Griffiths, Mr Holmes ... but how could you know?'

'The West Riding is a centre for clothing, and the demand for khaki uniforms in 1917 would be great, alas. The occupation is not an uncommon one, especially among women.'

Doyle took the prints from Holmes. 'Yet these figures are well executed for a girl,' he mused.

'The older girl is an artist of some promise,' confessed Gardner.

'And well able to copy,' added Holmes, reaching for a volume on his shelf entitled *The Princess Mary Gift Book* and actually signed by the royal patron herself. 'One of the volumes I bequeathed to our lawyer, Waston, who values such signatures. It was first brought out in 1914 and enjoyed a huge circulation and would likely be to hand in the household.' He leafed briefly through the children's book. 'Ah, here we are. This illustration by Shepperton to Noyes' poem clearly bears a resemblance to your fairies, Gardner. The angle of the raised leg here is almost identical.'

I marvelled, yet again, at the astounding memory of my friend. It must have been years since he had looked through the book and yet . . .

Doyle grunted as he compared the illustration with the fairy photograph. 'You're right again, Holmes. And, I see, there is an article by me in this book too, by God. I should have spotted it.'

'Other urgent matters claimed your valuable time,' consoled the detective. 'The *Strand* will have to do without the Cottingley fairy photographs for sure.'

Gardner looked pathetically crestfallen. 'I really do apologize for taking up your time, Mr Holmes. And yours, of course, Dr Watson. And, Sir Arthur . . .' He paused dolefully.

Holmes smiled, putting a friendly arm round his shoulder. 'Never fear, dear sir, never fear. What is the motto of your society? "There is no religion higher than truth?"'

'It is indeed, Mr Holmes.'

The detective cast a thoughtful yet penetrating eye at Doyle. 'But, after all, as we know, this is only fiction. Had it been real life, it all might have been very different.'

[Watson's manuscript ends abruptly here.]

And, as we know, it *was* different, for there was no Sherlock Holmes on hand to solve the matter so readily.

Only, as now, humans and their imperfections.

❧ Appendix ❧

A Moral from Elsie Hill: The Long Blether

by Gabriel and the Devil
(With a beautiful voice chipping in from time to time)

G abriel and the Devil found themselves tagging along behind the planet Earth, as they took a flying stroll together around the sun one day.

The Devil pointed an accusing finger at Earth as it spun jauntily in front of them.

'There have been some queer goings on on that little globe of late.'

'Yes,' said Gabriel.

'I've had my eye on that little lot for some time now.'

Here the Beautiful Voice chipped in saying, 'I know what you are about to say, it is quite true that covetousness, whether it be riches or land or other's intelligence envying what others have has always been the main sin since human life began there.'

'There are many other sins,' said the Devil.

'And it's going to be too bad for some,' said Gabriel.

The Beautiful Voice went on, 'They do not realize that the well-being of each human being depends on the behaviour of the rest of the human race. In the whole history of the earth planet there has never been anything as bad as what recently took place in Germany when they were led by one little big headed paper hanger in his fits of mad jealousy to destroy seven million quite goodliving brilliant and artistic people, and their Christian churches hardly lifted a finger to stop it. Germany knew what was happening – they had envied the Jews for so long they just didn't care, but chose to grab and murder. The churches could have closed saying no more christenings, weddings or funerals until this hounding and murder of the Jews ends.'

'They probably thought Jesus looking down would be pleased,' said the Devil.

'After all it was only a small group of his fellow Jews who condemned him to the cross nearly 2000 years ago. He understood this and forgave them,' said Gabriel.

'Yes,' said the Devil,' but if another Hitler character were to get a hold on any other country on that little globe, he could organize torture and persecution on the same grand scale. He would find fanatics who hated this or that political or religious creed, and he could find among the Mafia in Italy and America, and among the bull torturers in Spain, and in Britain the child beaters and their football fanatics and those who kill to steal.'

'Yes,' said Gabriel, 'speaking of the Mafia, at least the Italians let their children grow up before some of them get battered and end up in a slab of concrete – it's an unheard of thing for a child to get battered.'

'Another lot of recruits he would find would be the British hospital workers who thought it was right to engage in industrial warfare against the old and the sick, cutting off heat and food and medical supplies in the depth of winter, over a time keeping dispute. Also the two opposing sections in Northern Ireland who kill and cripple indiscriminately,' said the Devil.

'I was interested in your remark,' said Gabriel, 'about the well-being of each and every man being the well-being of the whole, for I think some are beginning to realize at last that the whole world is made very like one human being – a hurtful disease on one part of the body can cause far flung pains in other places.'

'Yes,' said the Beautiful Voice, 'twice tear-saddened eyes from all over the world turn towards Germany, the first ones from Jewish virgins who were sterilized by the thousand by German doctors, and then from Germany came the thalidomide babies. When they sterlized the young Jewish women they believed they were doing the right thing and later when they made the pill they thought it was going to be beneficial too. Now hundreds of mothers of thalidomide children all over the world must turn tragic faces to the same place where so many young women were sterilized and deprived of ever having a baby.'

'And here's another thing they have never pondered on,' said the Devil, 'it was a woman Jewish scientist who had escaped from Germany who produced the one last vital link in the splitting of the atom. It was a long way from the festering sore around Hitler but like a hurtful boil whose poison in the blood stream had to erupt somewhere. Hiroshima in fact.'

'One would have thought,' said the Devil, 'it should have been Germany.'

'No,' said the Beautiful Voice. 'The Gestapo camps had to be seen by the rest of the people on earth. The backlash comes in so many ways. Take the sad little smoke signals for help that went up from hundreds of Red Indian settlements as they starved to death, after the main source of protein had been killed off by the white man who shipped tons of buffalo skins to far off parts of the world leaving the carcasses to rot in the sun, and so many cold meatless winters for the starving and dying Indians. But probably not one Indian ever died with lung cancer from tobacco smoking as tobacco was used in a pipe and mostly only on ceremonial occasions, but the Indians' tobacco discovery caught on in a big way, over a large part of the world, and when it finally got rolled up into hundreds of millions of cigarettes, lung cancer started in a big way.'

'Yes,' said the Beautiful Voice, 'it would be interesting to check up how this has evened out. The deaths from both causes, the Red Indians who died of starvation, and the deaths up to date from the tobacco habit acquired from them, and there still will be enough smoke going up from cigarettes to make a gigantic smoke signal each year for a very long time yet.'

'I noticed there is one big subject you let smoke get in your eyes over,' said the Devil, 'a very burning subject. What about those two young bucks, New Russia and fairly New America dancing round each other and flexing their nuclear muscles.'

'True,' said the Beautiful Voice. 'They are both very young and very touchy, neither of them can bear any criticism.

'And the droll thing is,' said Gabriel, 'they both look alike. The strong hard-working strain of the first Russia pioneers who left their home land for America shows in a percentage in the faces of white Americans today. Walk down any street in Moscow or Chicago and you will see the three pure Russian type features. Well, there is your answer – a father and son with the same stubborn temperament never get on together.'

'Though sometimes,' said the Beautiful Voice, 'once the mother points out the cause of the friction to the father, his ego simmers down and things between father and son get better even though they still differ on vital subjects.'

The Beautiful Voice then acquired a jocular tone and said, 'I'll toss you for who has to play Mother!'

The Devil then became quite savage and angry saying, 'Shut up and keep your place and just remember that I am the ambassador of this little planet at present and all you two can do is to keep strictly to your path walking right behind me.'

'You might,' said the Beautiful Voice, 'wind up with only a ball of ashes in your hands. It's a well known gossip all over the Universe that the Earth has enough nuclear bombs to whip around it three times.'

'Yes,' taunted Gabriel, 'and then you would be out of a job.'

'And,' said the Beautiful Voice, 'you would not get a chance to approach any other galaxy with that kind of recommendation, would you?'

'Let's get on to a lighter subject,' said Gabriel. 'Now I remember once zooming down to a spot during the second war. It was a place that had once been a well known botanical garden but now I found it a blood-strewn mess where guns had been blasting ... everything gone and only frayed tree stumps, and on one half remaining tree a notice board hanging on one nail, bearing these words PICKING FLOWERS PROHIBITED. Beneath it were soldiers, broken bodies sprawled in churned up mud.'

'Really!' said Gabriel. 'You have got to laugh.'

At this the Beautiful Voice became stern and angry. 'I don't see anything funny about that at all. What I do feel convinced about is that they had better start nailing notice boards on every tree all over the world with these words:

'ALL FOR EACH OTHER OR ALL FOR THE NEXT WORLD.'

❧ Source Material ❧

Source Material

Books

Charles Kingsley, *The Water Babies* (Macmillan, 1863)

Maurice Maeterlinck, *The Unknown Guest* (Methuen, 1913)

Princess Mary's Gift Book (Hodder & Stoughton, 1915)

E. Bozzano, *Discarnate Influence in Human Life* (International Institute for Psychical Research, London, n.d.)

Arthur Conan Doyle, *The Coming of the Fairies* (Hodder & Stoughton, 1922)

Geoffrey Hodson, *Fairies at Work and Play* (Theosophical Publishing House, 1925)

Arthur Conan Doyle, *At the Edge of the Unknown* (John Murray, 1930)

Edward L. Gardner, *Fairies: A Book of Real Fairies* (Theosophical Publishing House, 1945)

Robert Payne, *The Great Charlie* (Andre Deutsch, 1952)

Cyril Scott, *The Boy Who Saw True* (Nevill, 1953)

Katharine Briggs, *A Dictionary of Fairies* (Allen Lane, 1976)

Charles Higham, *The Adventures of Conan Doyle* (Norton, New York, 1976)

H. O. Yardley, *The History of a Poker Player* (Fontana, 1980)

Peter Brookesmith, Introduction to *When the Impossible Happens* (Orbis, 1984)

Ann Petrie, *Your Psychic World A to Z: An Everyday Guide* (Arrow, 1984)

Fred Gettings, *A Dictionary of Astrology* (Routledge, 1985)

Articles

Arthur Conan Doyle, (*Strand*, Dec. 1920) pp.463–8

Arthur Conan Doyle, (*Strand*, Mar. 1921) pp.199–206

Edward L. Gardner, 'Elementals' (*Prediction*, Oct. 1947)

P. Chambers, 'At last I know the truth about Tinkerbell' (*Daily Express*, 24 May 1965)

Stewart F. Sanderson, 'Presidential address to the Folklore Society. The Cottingley Fairy photographs: a reappraisal of the evidence' (*Folklore*, vol. 84, Summer 1973)

Walter Clapham, 'There *were* fairies at the bottom of the garden' (*Woman*, 25 Oct. 1975)

'Feedback. A fairy story' (*New Scientist*, 10 Aug. 1978)

Peter Holdsworth, 'Fairy Godmother is so bewitching' (*Bradford Telegraph and Argus*, 21 Oct. 1978)

Joe Cooper, 'The Case of the Cottingley Fairies' (*Unexplained*, no. 20, Jan./Feb. 1981)

Joe Cooper, 'The reappearance of the fairies' (*Unexplained*, no. 21, Jan/Feb. 1981)

Joe Cooper, 'The Cottingley Fairies revisited' (*Unexplained*, no. 22, Jan/Feb. 1981)

Fred Gettings, 'Once upon a time' (*Unexplained*, no. 116, Dec. 1982)

Joe Cooper, 'Cottingley – At last the truth' (*Unexplained*, no. 117, Jan. 1983)

Geoffrey Crawley, 'That astonishing affair of the Cottingley Fairies' (*British Journal of Photography*, Dec. 1982, Apr. 1983. Concluded May 1985, July 1986)

Peter Holdsworth, 'Famous fairies *do* exist insists Frances' (*Bradford Telegraph and Argus*, 18 Sept. 1984)

Television Features

BBC *Nationwide* (17 Nov. 1971 and Nov. 1976)

ITV *Magpie* (11 July 1975)

Yorkshire TV (Sept. 1976)

BBC 2 *Play of the Week, Fairies* by Geoffrey Case (27 Sept. 1978)

❧ Index ❧

FROM THE ACADEMY AWARD-WINNING PRODUCER OF 'FORREST GUMP'
AND THE ACADEMY AWARD-WINNING PRODUCER OF 'BRAVEHEART'

FAIRYTALE
A TRUE STORY

COMING TO A CINEMA NEAR YOU

ICON ENTERTAINMENT INTERNATIONAL PRESENTS

An ICON PRODUCTIONS/WENDY FINERMAN production A CHARLES STURRIDGE film "FAIRYTALE – A TRUE STORY" FLORENCE HOATH ELIZABETH EARL PAUL McGANN PHOEBE NICHOLLS HARVEY KEITEL PETER O'TOOLE

Music by ZBIGNIEW PREISNER Edited by PETER COULSON Costume Designer MICHAEL HOWELLS Director of Photography MICHAEL COULTER B.S.C. Production Designer PAUL TUCKER Story by ALBERT ASH & TOM McLOUGHLIN and ERNIE CONTRERAS

Screenplay by ERNIE CONTRERAS Produced by WENDY FINERMAN and BRUCE DAVEY Directed by CHARLES STURRIDGE